NOW YOU KNOW

CHRISTOPHER CHASE WALKER

Acorn Independent Press

Published by Acorn Independent Press Ltd, 2012.

ISBN 978-1-908318-50-3

www.acornindependentpress.com

To Brown Jo

With much love + thanks
for the French words that
appear in here, and for
everything at 194

To Mary

Chris

For M—

one

His name was M—.

M: it was stamped in scarlet on his cardinal-coloured pullover. It was written in black on his birth certificate – and again, now, you have to think, scribbled on some anonymous slip of a form recording his unlamented death. And it was there, of course, all over the news, in the chat rooms, on the blogs and social networking sites that heralded his feats – or disparaged him. M: it was on everyone's lips. You couldn't miss him that spring and summer when his star, loaded with such dazzling gravity, lifted our hearts. Everyone knew him. Or really, everyone knew of him.

But nobody knew him better than me. And his name was M—.

Mum and I lived next door to his family, but I don't believe anyone knew the sort of person he was or would come to be – nobody could. He was so unremarkable that if you passed him on the pavement, you would instantly forget anyone had been there. Jammed in front of him on a packed train, you'd be unaware he was standing right behind you, only inches away. It was the way he breathed, almost as though he didn't want to take anything more than his share, for he was thin beyond belief. He would only use up so much space, so much air. He took little and gave nothing away. I didn't even know his name for more than a year after we moved in.

When I say that Mum and I lived next door to his family, what I really mean is that he and I lived next door to each other. We were neighbours; we became friends of sorts. Maybe I wasn't invited round more than two or three times, maybe I never so much as set foot on his stairwell, but I know it for fact that his bedroom was adjacent to mine. Only a foot of terraced Victorian brick separated us – and separated me from the low, mournful noises M— made for over a week after the crime scene tape was torn down and the reflective-vested police disappeared from his front garden. Crime, whether or not we like to admit it, is fixed squarely to our lives. Muggings, murders, rapes, burglaries, carjacks, hold-ups, assaults, bombs – they're all there, waiting to leap out like some scabby fox just as soon as you turn your back. But, in our corner of leafy south London you never expected anything right next door.

And M—, even if he never said as much to me, never expected it in his own home. Imagine!

I suppose word must have got round about his parents being an easy target. Don't get me wrong, it's not like they were that elderly, but it's also not like you can see them putting up a fight. Their back door wasn't locked with so much as a chain in the hours they were awake. They didn't own much – not even a car – and all that was stolen during the break-in was whatever cash happened to be at hand, some electronics worth barely enough to fill a pipe.

If only it had stopped there.

If only *they* had stopped there.

But they didn't.

There were three of them and not one of them stopped. They knife M—'s mum. Her arms, her back, her chest and legs. Hands. In the face. Deep, razoring cuts. M—'s father is beaten to death. Lumps like a rash of cricket balls swelling all over his head. Shatter his jaw, his hands. Kneecaps. His spine. And Tara... poor Tara is torn to bits. Tara was M—'s girlfriend, a tiny twist of a thing with dark hair straight down her back and eyes like crop circles. Her body, according to the news, was found 'away from the others'. I knew about Tara from the papers, but it was only the last time M— and I spoke, months later, at summer's end, that he mentioned her to me.

I remember it. Clear as day, I remember it. Watching me fill the kettle he said, 'That's why she was there that night. We were going to announce we planned to ... '

More than a minute later you could hear the weight of M—'s self-reproach when he said, as though he were speaking not to me but apologising to Tara, 'And I was late. I was late.'

If it had been silent before he had spoken – if, by then, I'd grown used to the long gaps between whatever he deemed important enough to vocalise, to his eclipse-like absences that could last for days and days – it was nothing like the quiet that followed this confession. Words, like everything else about M—, like the small swallows of air he rationed his unchallenged lungs, always slipped sparingly from him in something no less benign than a whisper.

But when he told me about Tara, the words plucked at my skin. Pinch, pinch – *ow!* It was something to do with all that M—, however thinly or moderately, had already revealed to me in the months since the murders (since we first came to know each other beyond the nod and the wave). I didn't know which surprised me more: that M— had been planning to marry or that he had waited so long before telling me he had planned to marry. I'd never seen Tara while she was alive, and it's my great shame that when M— told me they'd been engaged I couldn't think of a thing to say. Not a bloody thing. I try to convince myself that this satisfied him in some strange sort of way, that he wasn't offended, and that he'd probably deliberated even mentioning his engagement until he saw I was unlikely to explode with lamentations.

But I wish I'd responded. I wish I'd said something.

You know what I *did* do? I handed him a mug of tea.

Stephen – I'm okay to call you Stephen, aren't I? None of this 'Mr Fry' business if I know you – he tells me his girlfriend gets murdered the night they were to announce their engagement and all I can do is sling him a tea!

M— stirred in a few grains of sugar, a drop of milk. Minutes later he went away. It's true you still hear about him. The people he rescued, the criminals he caught (and the ones who vanished), and all the terrible things he did to them. But it was the last time I would see him. Ever.

The world has changed.

My world has changed.

I've changed. *God*, have I changed. If it's for the better, I don't know. I like to think so, but I really don't know. Who am I to say? If I can say anything at all it's that I've got everything straight these days. Everything straight in my head. And I can talk about it. You wouldn't believe how much I've wanted to. You wouldn't believe how many times I've gone over everything in my head. Six years of it. Six. Years. Every day for six years, since when I was an all-but-jailbait and jail-bound seventeen, I've been practising what to say.

Practise, practise, practise.

It's a means to an end, I suppose.

I'm just glad it's you I get to tell. This ... this *chanson de geste*.

two

There was nothing odd about the night M—'s parents and girlfriend were killed, nothing sinister. Your typical Monday. Flat. Lifeless. Nothing telling, nothing extraordinary or peculiar or … What I really mean is that there was nothing signalling they were about to die. But you've got to imagine it was one of those dizzying, hold-onto-your-hat evenings for M—, all but spilling over with the sort of emotion that percolates inside you when – and *this* is a wild guess – when you're about to announce something as monumental as getting married. It would have been like a bodily giggle in his rangy gait and in the way his long and nimble fingers, accustomed to pitter-pattering at the keypad in his office cubicle, must have twitched.

The air was still, the sun had long since dropped behind the houses sloping up toward the high street, and it was through my bedroom window that I heard the sirens. Yes, it might have been dark but don't ask me about the stars. Except M—; I doubt if anything shone as brightly as he. I can picture him, as crisp and thin as a payslip, as he approached home in the warm evening air, bubbling away inside with the confection of his announcement, with the tedious delay at London Bridge, the overcrowded train ride … and suppressing everything to a sharp little flicker in his huge, cow-like eyes.

His eyes.

That flicker. *God, that flicker*. How he must have wished and wished it had been the eyeflash – the great bursts of light – he would soon enough get in the corners of his eyes, like a sixth sense suddenly slamming in. The eyeflash that would have sent him flying home if only he already had it. The eyeflash he wouldn't have *ever* had if he hadn't come whistling up the front path something like forty minutes late that night. Moment he steps through his front door and – BANG! – cracked across the face with a baseball bat, carving him right open to the beast up here, in his head, that that very second twitched into life.

Or, perhaps, what he truly wished for was that none of it happened at all. That life, in its dullest everyday fashion, sloped and slipped along exactly as it had before. Yes, I bet that's just what he thought, just what he wanted. So, just imagine how it must have borne down on him, how it must have squeezed at his splintered heart that his eyeflash, his great ability to detect violence and danger in the coiled moments before they struck, his superpower, not only came too late but wouldn't have ever come at all if he hadn't lost everything that had once meant the world to him. And still did, even if they were dead.

I suppose he must have thought it was a curse.

What the rest of the world thought is different. But I don't, for a moment, believe that anyone – anyone apart from M— and I, of course – knew about his eyeflash. If I'm honest, I can't say I knew about it straight away. It was only after he had saved my life twice that I knew anything about it at all; he described it to me in his quiet, confessional way.

M— said it was an inward burst of light in his pupils or irises that would erupt without warning, specifically *to* warn. It all but blinded him. It let on nothing to anyone but him, no matter how hard you looked. And so only he could know its true purchase and sting.

M— was isolated. He was stranded. The eyeflash must have made him feel worlds away. Damned. A freak.

There was M— and then there was M. M— who lived next door, and the M who would be headline news. Do you follow? Do you see? Who he was and what he became. Nobody's going to tell me they weren't one and the same. Nobody.

I'm no good with being orderly. The facts, yes. *Definitely*, yes. But doing things exactly as they come, step by step, from A to Z … What

I'm saying is, in case I forget to say it later, thank you, Stephen. Thank you for having me round like this, for listening to me. Of all the people I could imagine … It's an honour. But, if it's okay, let's not call this an interview. Too stuffy, too formal; I'd be nervous and get all my answers wrong. A 'chat' is more like it. Just two good people sat opposite each other, talking. Tea. Biscuits. A stuffed armchair, a chaise longue … it's how I've always pictured it.

So. Right. The first time I had so much as an inkling of M—'s superpower, if we should even call it a superpower, was in April, three or four weeks or so after his parents and girlfriend were killed. I'd finished revising the essay on which I'd hung my hopes of – well, what's the point? I dropped all of my coursework sometime after M— disappeared and I didn't see the point of ever going back. But, that afternoon, I was still the determined student. Quids in, as Mum would say. Having fired off an electronic copy of my essay to my tutor at the last minute, I was obliged to submit two hard copies by post. In my haste and apprehension, I forgot to enclose the signed declaration that all the work was mine. I don't suppose I would have ever known about M—'s eyeflash at all if a light bulb hadn't suddenly gone off in my head. Halfway to the high street and – *ping!* – I remembered the declaration and hurried home to collect it. Then I sped back up the road, and it was only when I was nearing the postbox and thinking about what I'd like to do next that I saw M— and …

You'll shake your head, Stephen. You'll remind me how Oscar Wilde called it a 'tax on stupidity' – by the way, I thought you nailed it in *Wilde*. You *were* him. I must have watched it a hundred times – but, when I saw M—, I was thinking I'd treat myself to three scratchcards: a Diamond Life, maybe a Squids o'Plenty, a Royal Flush or … any would do, just so long as there were three. Three was good luck: one for each copy of my essay.

M— though. I don't think I would have noticed him if it wasn't for the purple bruising across his eyes, like a glossy carnival mask. Some people – I don't want to be mistaken for racist – but some people can look like everybody else. Ordinariness as a disguise.

It was him, though. That's the important point. I was at the postbox on the corner and I called his name. But, before I could so much as wave, M— swooped over and shoved me with such a might that you'd never expect from someone so punishingly thin, sending me flapping like a talent show dancer into the fresh fruit crates in front the grocer's. I slipped on a grape and fell on a mango. Splat! Flat on my arse. Looking up, I caught a glimpse of the dented white van that had hopped the kerb. It hurtled round the corner. Tyres squealing, engine gunning, the works. Like on telly.

M— rubbed his eyes as though they'd come unstuck. I remember him groaning – a soft, almost accidental groan that I later realised sounded like the noise cats make when they yawn. He said nothing; it took some doing before the grocer, all lungs and writhing moustache, cooled off, finally (and rather reluctantly, I'll admit) conceding it was possible M— hadn't been defending himself from me. We had to pay him for his ruined produce. Or rather, I handed over my £3 scratchcard money and M— had to pay everything else. I had my lucky 50p piece on me, but I wasn't about to give *that* away. The strawberries and bananas and lychee and melons and everything else split and oozing on the pavement were how I would have looked if it hadn't been for M—. All of it was too damaged to even think about carting home. DOA. I promised to pay M— back.

Yes, it was April, I'm certain of it. Easter Monday. Apart from the Chicken Cottage, the Pizza Kebab, the shop doing 'American' nails, the pub, the bookies, the pound store, and the off-license, the only place open was Costcutters, who were doing slow trade in chocolate eggs. I would have bought one for M— if I hadn't had to fork out all my pocket money on the fruit, and if I'd thought about it at the time. I didn't. But it wasn't as though he celebrated Easter anyway.

Yes, it was April and it was bank holiday weekend and there were blossoms in the trees. Pink blossoms. Cherry blossoms. Magnolia. And birdsong. It couldn't have been more than three weeks since everything next door. A fortnight since, through the bedroom wall, I last heard M—'s broken and syrupy wail.

The funerals were held only days after the murders. Three or four or something like that: custom for you. M—'s sprawling net of aunts and uncles and cousins and half-relatives and god-knows-who-else packed the place. Some of them were probably so far-flung that they must have been more like strangers to him than I was. They filled his house and the front and back gardens, commiserating with him and with each other. I watched everything from my bedroom window, from the kitchen window and from the sitting room. Even peeked out the back door into the garden once or twice. But did I see M—? Hardly. He wasn't in shape for a party. His eyes were blackened and he must have been incredibly sore. Knowing him, he probably kept out of the way or maybe even hid.

You could hardly blame him: the house was filled with everyone he knew; you don't have to be the King of Mensa to see how that would only remind him of just who wasn't there.

But now that I think about it ... I don't know, I really don't know. Now that I think about it, trying to set the record straight, I'm not so sure how swiftly the funerals *were* held. Knowing the undisguised look of resentment Mum could make, and how she had probably trained this on M— and his parents, it's no surprise we weren't invited to the funerals or the gathering next door that, in other circles, you'd call a wake. And there's every reason to think the coroner must have held onto the bodies for days longer than is custom for anyone whose tradition is to bury their dead lickety-split.

Regardless, whenever it was, there was definitely a big do next door. Food like it was a wedding feast. Families came by the droves. And through the windows (and through the walls) you could hear voices and the sounds of what, believe it or not, were Abba songs playing – perhaps, I thought later, for the children. There were enough of them to open a crèche.

But one by one (and in pairs and by the half-dozen) they went away. Ten or eleven o'clock and M— was on his own. He was alone. Late that night, I heard him roaming about the house. It was as though he was trying not to make any noise and, in doing so,

made far more noise than he would have made ordinarily. M—
didn't drink, so I knew he wasn't crashing around drunk. You ask
me and it must have been his eyes. They were already swollen, but
now if he was crying too …

I hear him and I freeze. Stretch out my neck and, quiet as I can,
tip-toe closer to the wall and listen, listen. But the noises vanish.
Nothing but the drips and creaks houses always make. Incidental
ticks and taps, pipes clicking and tinkling as though nestling
down to sleep. I put my ear to the wall, but there's nothing there.
Crazy as it sounds, I put my hand to the wall, to about where I
imagined M—'s head would be if he were lying in bed just the
other side. I smooth the wall and, holding my breath, listen extra
hard: nothing, not a peep. It's only when I'm about to go to bed
myself that I see I'll never get so much as a wink if I don't take
a last look out the window, down at M—'s garden, to make sure
there's nothing sinister happening. Outrageous of me, maybe, but
I honestly wondered if the noises I'd heard were the murderers
coming back to finish the job.

I thought it was down to me to save M—'s life.

Outside was dark. Proper dark: almost inky. His garden was
and, for what it's worth, ours was too. Not a star in sight. Where
the moon was hiding was anyone's guess. M—'s kitchen door was
shut, the windows closed and all the lights were off. If there was
anything strange, it was that the gate at the end of his garden was
unlatched. The gate was fire engine red. It opened onto the ragged
copse that ran behind the houses along our side of the street. And
it creaked when it swung in the breeze.

On 22 March that year, Paul and Danielle Barnes were walking
home from dinner out. Pizza Express. It's eleven o'clock; there's a
wispy fog. A hooded gang attacks them in Rennison Close. There
is nowhere to run. Paul falls on the first punch. He dies from
multiple stab wounds 'by a long blade'. Danielle loses their baby.
And the tenner in her handbag.

On 27 March, around 9:30p.m., a group of hooded youths threw
a dog over the fifth floor balcony of Keats House, in the Hartley

Estate. The dog had been forced to fight; she is killed because she lost. Her injuries are near fatal before she is tossed. Witnesses hear her whimpering as she is dragged past their doors. Hear her yelp when she is lifted to the edge, scream as she falls seventy feet onto a cycle rack.

three

You ask me and there's nothing more tragic than a life hinged on something out of control. Your control, mine, anybody's. It's like … it's as though you're on the bus home and you're moving along, moving along, when you look up from your paper to discover you're circling and re-circling the same roundabout and there isn't a stop in sight. While that spring and summer were caught up with M— and, as the days grew longer and then shorter again, the gathering intensity and notoriety of his deeds, my own little life was captivating enough, even when it bored me barmy.

What I mean is there was a lot more going on than everything with M—, despite how much and how often I thought about him.

Most of my time I spent studying. Studying or throwing myself at some trifling, time-consuming activity that meant I didn't study as much as I intended or should. I watched telly. I played games on the PC. I drew pictures and patterns in my notebooks and knocked about on the Interweb, reading blogs and the BBC, the *Standard*, and everything people were saying about themselves on Facebonk and all that. I sat on the side of the bath sampling Mum's toiletries – cucumber wipes, apricot hand creams, sugary exfoliators … None of it posh or expensive or anything, just your basic high street stuff from Asda and Boots and the like. I flipped through my dictionary and read whole pages at random, writing down words I liked: new words, clever-sounding words, words whose definitions I thought I knew but couldn't have defined if asked. Erudite was a favourite. Tangential. Tertiary (you'll laugh, but I thought it had something to do with terrapins). Blouson. Celeriac. Confabulate. Calendrical. Mesmerical. Chimera. Pectoral. Pubis.

What else …? I went to the shops, won and lost on scratchcards, made lists: of books to read, films to watch, countries to visit when I went travelling. For at least a week, I went completely potty and obsessed over our back garden, your basic postage stamp of clay, weeds and building debris. Brambles, dandelions … the lot. I doubt if the whole thing measured twenty metres square, but it took me something like ten days to get it in shape. And whether on my knees, or just sat there covered in dirt with great mounds of garden waste crowded round me, I couldn't help but imagine M— was watching me with enough measure to register as approval. I figured he must have been given some time off work, 'compassionate leave' Mum called it, and, crazy as it sounds, I reckoned he could do no better than to watch me from his bedroom window.

Perhaps that's not so far-fetched? Perhaps bored or lonely or seeking solace from the springtime blossoms, he did see me. Perhaps he even nodded to himself over a cup of tea, looking on as I wrestled with metre after metre of the weeds that ran up the trees and spiralled along the sagging wooden slats of the trellises. Hardly an hour passed when I wouldn't catch myself looking for him over my shoulder.

But M— was never there. At least not that I saw. He was difficult enough to spot as it was.

More than anything, though, I would sit with my feet on the kitchen table, or over the arm of the sofa, staring at the electronic tag on my ankle. I would spend hours thinking about who was at the other end of its signal. Wondering: just how closely are they watching me? I had to be home by nine every night. That was my curfew. If I wasn't home by nine, the tag would signal to its monitor, and the monitor would signal whoever monitored monitor signals and whose job it was to promptly signal the police to haul me back to court, from where I'd be chucked in jail to be bullied, beaten and raped. I mean look at the size of me!

I sort of half-believed being tagged meant that somewhere someone knew when I so much as went to the loo or made a cuppa or turned over in bed, hot and swollen-eyed, desperate for sleep.

They would know when I wanked and, this all but killed me, let me tell you, who and what I thought about when I wanked.

Or so I thought, so I half-believed.

Barking.

If I ever need any artillery to argue the oppressiveness of believing in God, I only have to remember that rubbery black anklet with the look and feel of a sports watch: nothing snaps your spirit so certainly as being under constant anonymous surveillance. It's like being hunted. So, in a way, it's how M— must have felt. Only it was he who, chased by this restless internal determination, was the hunter. It was him in the shadows. He who appeared out of nowhere to save your life. Or take it.

But he didn't intend to do any of that. He happened into it. Stumbling, bungling, mistaking … No, no, *definitely.* I have to think M— was only after one thing; he was looking for *them.* Hunting the three: LOCK Crazy Crew.

I wonder if he knew he would disappear after he found them.

I wonder if he planned it that way.

I wonder what happened to him.

I wonder …

Mum didn't like it, but every evening I'd come home from the newsagent's with an armful of papers. For one pound fifty they'd let me have a copy of each of that day's unsold stock; I usually came home with five or six. Mum said they made the place a mess. I suppose she was right. But then mums are always saying things.

And so do the papers, of course. By and large they give you the same story, only tell it in all sorts of ways. Scoops here, quotes there. Some, as you know, are for the university-educated. Some have a local or political slant. Others, you're all but required to flip through at the caff whilst a bacon sarnie goes soggy on your plate. Me? I didn't care what I read: I'd read anything, I read everything. Strangest thing was when two or three papers reported on a story in another paper or something off the telly. News *was* news. Or rather news becomes news on a slow news day.

That's what I liked best about journalism: you can get away with practically anything. I thought there must be a place in it for me. Journalism (I might as well say it) was one of the two subjects I was studying by correspondence. The other was design. Not any particular sort of design, only the basics. How journalism and design relate to one another, I didn't know. Complete mystery. All I can say is I was interested in both and, after doing my GCSEs and leaving school, I didn't want to give up on me, so I studied journalism and design. Doing two subjects was a way of spreading my bets. Like the windows on scratchcards, I thought one would come up trumps.

The tag on my ankle meant I couldn't go anywhere – at least not at night – and it meant I wasn't getting anywhere with getting out and getting a place of my own anytime soon. But it couldn't stop me going places in my head. In that way, studying the news got me out of the house, away from Mum and into the world. Somewhere where I could forget about things, forget about me and forget I was hiding. Despite what I say about wasting my time, I worked hard at my studies. I drew and sketched until my fingers were stiff and my back would pop like bubble wrap when I un-hunched from over my desk late-late at night. When I saw a story in three or four different papers, when I saw it all over the telly or online, I'd hoover up all I could, piece things together, and then knock-up my own version. I spent hours at it. Hours reading, hours writing, hours trying to puzzle out the truth.

Anything really, I should admit, so I didn't have to face up to me. It doesn't make sense (it doesn't to me, not now), but like my tag meant I was all but jailed at night, there were things in my head that could keep me indoors for days and days. I sometimes thought that if I went out like I wanted to, everything would *come out*.

Any coming out was no good.

It scared me.

So I stayed in.

Call me crazy, but at the same time I was desperate to leave home. Ab-so-lutely desperate.

I knew I had the brains to make it on my own. It wasn't all the time I spent looking up words and trying them out – that was for fun. It was more to do with … I don't think there's any conceit in saying I was good at school. Maybe I left as soon as I could, but there were reasons for that. I was new there. We moved house when I was sixteen and I had to move school too. I didn't know anyone at the new place. I didn't have any friends. I did my studies, my grades were decent and … and it wasn't as though I didn't have any ambition or anything, but more that I simply wanted to leave. So I did, and enrolled in Westminster & City University's remote learning programme. I could study at my own pace, from home, without anyone around. Nobody guessing about me or my secrets.

And I really don't think there's anything big-headed about saying how clever I am either. I've got brains, I've got them all right. Maybe – probably – not as much as you but … I took six online IQ tests (one every other month for a year after I left school) and scored 122, 146, 118, 119, 141, and 137. That's an average of 130. It doesn't make me a genius – but then I never claimed to be. Not seriously, anyway. Put simply, it means I'm not just another baseball-capped chav chavving it up on package holiday to Ibiza or something. It means I know how to get to the bottom of things.

Like with everything going on locally.

Like with everything happening right next door.

Like with M—: my obsession.

Believe you me, I wasn't alone. Hardly. At the start, nobody thought to link any one person to the loose pattern of deeds that, whilst hardly heroic, were picked up here and again by the news for their uncommon note of civility and equanimity. Just a series of unconnected one-offs. I'll come to them. I will. I'll tell you everything. Only promise me you'll steel yourself. Because it's not pretty. It's pretty awful.

But what I'm trying to say is that it was only later, when things began to escalate, that you could see a story was mounting up, up and … and that one man was behind all of it. One man: M—. Anyone tells you it was someone else, any of these 'theorists' out there, you tell them to piss off. Do yourself a favour and tell them to piss right off.

When M— started wearing the cardinal-coloured top with the one letter on it that practically told the world his name, he was everywhere. And the story – *God*, Stephen – the story was like Lily Allen. Every-bloody-where.

And the story was this: nobody could tell you his name. Nobody knew who he was. Nobody could remember his face. Only the scarlet M.

And the scarred, broken bodies that trailed in his wake.

Much as I'd like to say I had something to do with breaking the story, I can't. Though none of it passed me by. None of it. Not. One. Bit. I can say this, not only because I followed everything obsessively, but also because, before things really took off, before M was *NEWS*, I kept a record of those little local news items that were out of the ordinary. Things like someone sticking up for a cornered stranger. Or someone stepping in when they saw a shopkeeper getting hassled. Or someone getting the shit kicked out of them for saying something to the wannabe 'gangstas' playing music tinnily on their mobiles and throwing their takeaway rubbish at you. I kept a record of all of this because I thought it would make me a better person, the kind of person I wanted to be when I grew up. And also, let's face it, let's be honest, because I had nothing better to do. I was stuck. Jimmy Stewart: *Rear Window*. You get the picture.

What I mean is I could see something was happening. Only it took me awhile before I knew exactly what.

M— though. Poor heartbroken fool. He must have had a clear sense of what he was doing. His purpose. And you have to think it came to him that very night, straight away after he came to in his front hall and, through his mask of bruises and blood-burst eyes, found his parents' bodies in the sitting room and Tara's 'away from the others' sliced and glistening like some sort of horrible salad.

Whenever it did come to him, he certainly took right to it. Along the way he ended up doing all the stuff that changed us for good. Sometimes that's all it takes. Don't you think? Just one person standing up and saying, 'That's enough – I'm not having it. Stop!'

Okay, maybe it sounds purple-prosey but, you ask me, M— was like the sun coming out from behind a swell of thunderclouds, making everything shimmer. Pretty much everything he did was accidental, situations he came across when he was out looking for the people who had slaughtered everyone he loved.

He was hunting for them – LOCK Crazy Crew.

And know what? I think he found them too.

On 5 April, Isobel Rhodes, 33, was asleep in bed. Around 2:00a.m. she hears a noise. It's coming from the kitchen; she lives alone, a garden flat in Bridgewater Terrace. Isobel hits the panic button beside the nightstand. The siren screams. But nobody hears her screams: sock down her mouth. She is beaten, half-strangled and raped. She is filmed. Isobel thinks there are three of them. Maybe four. Maybe more. All those hands and … They take some jewellery, her mobile. Forty pounds cash.

On 12 April, in Bardale Road, Marlon Fields, 24, was shot dead. It's 8p.m., the last fingers of sun still clawing at the sky. There are yummy-mummies and baby buggies about. Marlon has his hands in his pockets when he is shot. Back of the head. He was out to the shops for biscuits and milk. Press speculate it was gang-related. It was and it wasn't.

four

LOCK Crazy Crew were Lester, Ommie and Carl. They were the top dogs, commanding some two dozen or more foot soldiers. They were in charge and they were out of control. Lester and Carl were brothers – twins, some of the press speculated when their story hit the papers – and Ommie was the runt of the gang, around my size. Five foot six. I don't think it matters much, the colour of their skin (what colour were their baseball bats, the handles of their knives?). They were the sort who wore hoods over their heads and covered their faces with bandanas. You could see in their eyes that, but for this curdled self-justified rage, they were dead – if, by chance, you saw their eyes at all. They were the sort who come at you from behind, at night, all at once. Fear was the quid pro quo. You gave them your dignity, the notes in your pocket or purse, your virginity, your life. They gave you fear. If you lived, you lived in fear. Shame was extra; but sometimes they threw it in cheap.

If they had ever been brought to court for the murder of Tara and of M—'s parents, they weren't the sort who'd blame society for their crimes or say that they'd been 'failed by the system'. They were too far gone for that.

Far, far too gone.

Stratospheric. Like the stars.

Of all the things we know about them, we know that Ommie sang in the choir at the evangelical church his mother dragged him to twice weekly throughout his childhood; and that Lester and Carl, like Ommie (and like me, to be honest), were fatherless – but more about that later. All three had been excluded from school. All three had been inside, on remand, in Feltham, for any combination of assault, GBH, and possession. All three had, since long before M came after them with all the slit-eyed fury of a snake, been living in abandoned council blocks and boarded up houses. All three had been banned from Aristocrats, the night club on the high street; and also from the Cherry Tree and the Costcutters where they had beat and bottled a woman who 'disrespected' them by asking if they would please hurry up and pay the man at the till. And all three, according to everything in the news, were last seen alive wearing hooded tops. Lester's was black, oversized, with white gothic lettering across the front and back; Carl's was midnight blue, with a Yankees logo, stolen from a market stall only the day before; and Ommie's was tea-coloured and stank of deodorant and gear.

I like to think M— caught them unawares. It's the kind of thing they would have done, the kind of thing they did. I like to think there was, for each of them, a blinding moment when they saw that their comeuppance would be absolute, that it would be brutal. And I like to think they didn't cry, but that a wild, paralysing fear surfaced in their eyes when they understood exactly who it was who had come for them. That he existed purely to punish them. And that they were, in fact, the one reason he was there.

I like to think he told them so.

By the time he did find Lester, Ommie and Carl, M— was wearing what everyone called a superhero's costume. Some reports said he wore a mask. Some 'eyewitnesses' even claimed he sported a cape. But his outfit was hardly so extravagant or showy. It was like him – understated and very nearly missable, just a top he wore beneath his coat. Only the criminals or their intended victims ever saw it – and then only at the last minute or by chance. What surprises me most is that M—'s coat, a long, dark high street version of the coats you see flash young bankers wearing in the City, had buttons right up to his throat. It wasn't as though he could just unzip it to reveal his top: he had to work at the buttons.

But then his fingers were always quick.

Without revealing where he actually worked, I think it's worth saying that M— did work in the City. Or at least he worked in an office somewhere on the outskirts of the City, and for a bank whose headquarters were in one of those concrete carbuncles that blemish the ... the *noblesse* of the old stone architecture you see everywhere in the Square Mile. He wasn't a banker, or your typical City boy. Not at all. No flash, no attitude, not a millimetre of greed. He was unassuming, a nine-to-five man and, in fact, what some people would call a nerd. He might have been a librarian or a bookbinder, if he hadn't been such a whiz at IT. Doing what exactly was never all that clear, at least not to me. You'd understand what he did if I could tell you. All that circuit board server router spyware firewall USB gigabyte dork talk is right up your alley.

But yes, M— did well for himself. I have to believe his parents were incredibly proud of him. He was their only child, respectful, about as noisy as a grape, and built like a foldaway bike. At 32 or 33, he was still living happily in their home.

Some people will think that's strange. But then some people have different customs. Besides, I don't think M—'s parents had much money. His father was retired and his mum had never worked. They probably counted on him to help pay the mortgage and utilities and to keep the place up to scratch. From the outside, it was immaculate. The masonry and windows were cleaned twice annually, roof was moss-free, and their privet hedge, cut square, was firm and crisp and an alarming shade of green. I think they must have fed it. And I know for fact the red bricks of their house were cleaner and more right-angled than ours. Everything was sturdy, well-mannered and tidy.

What they must have made of our garden, I hate to think. Mum would sometimes speak insultingly about M— and his family. She would say things about *them lot*, *they* and *that sort*. At first, I tried telling her she was simply envious of what they had (they owned, we rented) and of how they looked after things. But, after a while, I gave up and ignored her whenever she got sarcy about them. I reckon her resentment must have shown in her eyes, even her skin. It must have been obvious to M— and his parents what she made of them and why.

You can imagine my surprise then, when one evening M—
rang our buzzer. It was a first. He was fidgety, like it was a struggle
to keep calm. I thought something else must have happened,
something terrible. But it was only that he was locked out. He'd lost
his mobile he explained, patting the pockets of his suit jacket to
prove it, and asked if I minded ringing a locksmith. He apologised
if he was disturbing me (he wasn't – or rather he was, but not in
the way he meant). He spoke quietly and, if I remember, twice
used the word 'please'.

This was maybe a week or more after he'd pushed me out of
the van's way, and getting on for eight in the evening. It was only
later I saw that M— must have timed coming round for when he
thought Mum would definitely be home from work. He would
want another adult there. No trouble or insinuation that way.
But it was a Thursday and Mum was out. Or was it a Wednesday?
Doesn't matter. It was probably Ladies' Night in some cocktail bar
somewhere and Mum would have walked through a mist of Dior
and be in her best leggings and heels and out with 'the girls' from
her office or … wherever.

But back to M—. When I saw it was him this unbelievable
thrill raced through me. Do you know it? *God*, it's like a sparkler
going off inside: fizzing and crackling and hot to the touch. Mad,
completely mad. Frightening.

But delicious most of all: we were alone.

'I'll put the kettle on,' I told him, almost keeping my voice
steady. 'While you dial.'

M— said he didn't want to be any bother. He just stood there,
on our doorstep, hands in pockets, looking a total wreck. I told
him there were biscuits. I told him there were *chocolate* biscuits.
M— looked over his shoulder at his house and stared. His long,
bare neck twisted so you could see his veins, the quickness of his
pulse. There was a moment when I thought he'd frozen. But then
he turned to me and said: 'Could …? Do you think …? Could I
check something, please? It's only that …'

He explained there might be a way in through the back. He
didn't ask me as much (he didn't ask me to do anything in fact),

but before he finished explaining things I told him I'd happily give it a go.

I *was* happy. Stephen, I was … *God*, it wasn't so much that he'd saved my life and I wanted to repay him in some way (I still didn't have the money I owed him – or really I'd nicked the money from Mum's handbag but then blown it on scratchcards), but more that there was something absolutely *gorgeous* about M—, something that made you go dizzy. Part of it was the way he dressed, always so sharply, in fitted shirts, striped silk ties and, at that time of year, in creamy, cropped linen suits. Part of it was how he held himself erect despite all that must have borne down on him. His hair, black and cut short, had buoyancy and sheen. But I really think it was his eyes. Maybe it's just me, but his eyes were this Marmite-and-butter brown that looked all the more beautiful and broken and round and moist and … *mesmirical* when you noticed how long his lashes were. M— blinking was like him beckoning you to come and have a look inside, to come right up close and have a jolly good look. And so, without having to look at him, but knowing all the same how he must have looked looking at me, I told him I would help and stood aside to let him in.

Before we made it as far as the kitchen it was all I could do not to reach out and touch his hand.

Now, I don't think it's always been true, but I suppose if I had to describe or classify myself I would say that I'm *reasonably* good-looking. Reasonably. I'm the same now as I was then. I'm not fat. Not too tall or midgety. There's nothing disastrous about my teeth. Or my breath: hoping to break my duck and score my first kiss, I'd given up smoking when I was fourteen, a full three years before that evening M— came round and showed me how to break into his house. And I like to think there's something people find attractive about my mouth. When I was a lot younger, when Dad was still around, it looked unnaturally wide and slack, as though my tongue would, at any second, come tumbling out like a carpet. But I grew into it. Now my tongue fits perfectly – and not just in *my* mouth! My hair is the same now as it was when I knew M—. Not blonde but sandy (as you see). A No. 2 all over. A suedehead.

I must have looked incredibly boyish to M—. I look at the photos I have from then and it's as though I'm looking at the distant past.

I only have two photos.

One is my mugshot: my probation officer gave me a copy at our final meeting. He said he thought it would remind me of the person I was and where I was and who and everything I wanted to become.

He was right.

The other photo is of M— and me. We're not doing anything in particular, only standing in our gardens. It's just the two of us and in that way it's always been immeasurably special. Both photos are only a few years old but, even still, I look at them and I see me as a child. Or caught somewhere between childhood and who I am today. Which of course I was.

Trapped, I suppose you could say.

But – where was I? Yes, when I broke into M—'s at his instruction, it was one of those spring evenings when you notice how long the days are growing. BST and all that. I can't remember what I was doing when M— rang our buzzer, probably not much. Coursework, watching some travel programme or another, doodling, or fannying about and eating this and that, like I always did when Mum wasn't home to make us dinner. What I do remember is that we'd had a sudden thunderstorm earlier that evening. I remember not so much because it bucketed it down and I had to race about shutting windows, but more because when I opened the door and saw M—, he looked so incredibly crisp and dry against the dripping trees and hedges, the glistening street and cars. You could smell the dust pelted off the pavement and scattered in the air. Ozone.

It was the same in the garden. There were pools of water and worms lolling about like drunken … like worms. I was careful not to tread on them, for I knew M— would be careful about that type of thing. I didn't want to do anything that would upset or trouble him. I didn't want to kill anything or stain his floors. He couldn't take any more of that.

From our garden I could just make out the uppermost panels of M—'s lean-to. This is important: his lean-to. It was a pristine and slant-roofed extension off the back of his house. I could only make out the top of it because there was a high wooden fence between our gardens. M— was older than me by more than a dozen years and he was also taller, by half a foot or more. When he pointed at the lean-to's little transom window with the broken latch that he thought I might be able to squeeze through, I had to grip the fence, stand on my toes and crane my neck to see it. It wouldn't be easy: although the transom was only something like six feet from the ground, it was above a glass door, itself set within a wall of thin glass. There were spades and rakes and forks and a whole B&Q of garden furniture stacked tidily inside. It was a simple storage structure and the transom looked as tight as a noose.

But I said I would do it.

And I did.

M—, had he been watching me the whole time, would have seen the electronic tag when I slid in headfirst and my jeans rode right the way up my shins. But, if he did see it, he didn't mention it. We didn't quiz each other. I didn't ask him anything like 'Where did it happen?' or 'They came through the kitchen door, right?' and he didn't say anything about my tag.

I also tried not to ask him about the little box room. I had to pass through it to get to the front door. First the lean-to, then through some French doors with frosted glass panes, then through the little box room and yet another door, up and along the narrow hall all but dripping with framed family photographs and pictures of George Harrison and Princess Diana, before finally letting in M— through his own front door. It was strange – really-*really* strange. Not his house, but the little box room. Scrubbed and bare but for this noisy red wallpaper that seemed to fill the whole of the room's empty space. I stared round for a moment, standing in the centre and holding out my arms to try and touch the walls. I couldn't, but it struck me how absolutely odd it was that such a pointless little room hadn't been knocked through or was left uncluttered with Hoovers and shoeboxes and shelving and all that. There wasn't even any dust! Apart from the French doors, it was windowless. I figured it must have been a scullery of some sort way back when. It certainly wasn't used for anything now.

I only stayed for a moment. Any longer, I worried, and it would look like I was snooping.

No, I left straight off.

Pretty much, at any rate.

M— shook my hand when I let him in. He smiled at me. And then something – well, then something *queer* happened. M— said he'd make us a cup of tea. My curfew was coming up fast, but was I about to say no! Just gulp it and go. As we headed toward the kitchen, I heard M— jut off suddenly and shut the door of the little box room with a smart little bang. When I started to ask him why he didn't use it for anything, M— looked away, up at the ceiling, as though there was a message written in the air. For a moment it was like he'd forgotten I was there. But then, with the wry grin he would sometimes share with you and could just about break your heart, he said: 'It's the wallpaper.'

I thought it must oppress him. And I had it on the tip of my tongue to say so, too. But I had a feeling he wasn't telling me something. So I kept my mouth shut.

I'm glad I did. When I think about that little box room now, I can almost smell the disinfectant and bleach. And I can picture everything I would soon find there – picture it in a heap, smouldering for a second at best, before the flames lick up and hold.

five

There had been a series of break-ins running up to Christmas, a series of break-ins and attacks. Horrible stuff. The worst. People beaten to death or their teeth knocked in. Rapes. People too frightened to stay in their homes. Or go outdoors. None of it was in our street, but all of it was local: around the corner, near the Montessori, in front of the little brick church that became a mosque, alongside the hilltop park, in the playground behind the hair salon, outside the pub where the night bus stopped. The police twice came to our door, appealing for witnesses. Had we seen anything? Heard the screams? Could they look in our garden? Were we okay? There were police outside the train station and on the buses, in helmets and hi-vis jackets and they stepped up foot patrols. Would that make us feel more secure? Mum bought locks for the windows, a second bolt for the back door. She rang and rang and rang the landlord until he fitted a panic button in her bedroom. She said she didn't expect I'd be much protection if someone broke in.

Mum was right. And she'd still be right today. I'm useless with that sort of thing. Look at my arms. I might as well be twelve!

But perhaps 'series' is the wrong word. A number is better: there had been *a number* of break-ins and attacks. But unless something happened to you yourself, or someone you knew, it was just something that happened, just another incident in the news. Frightening, but you forgot about it by the time you got to wherever you were going or woke up the next morning. Sometimes, from the bus, you would see groups of spectators gathered on the pavement in front of a house, a shop, a school, or in the dead gardens of some grim council block or other. Sometimes you might even see one or two groups of onlookers a week … and, a few days later, a bright yellow Witness Appeal sign would be whacked up, a slumping pile of cellophaned flowers would appear. But none of it seemed connected, never seemed to be more than you'd expect to see every now and again, living where we lived.

Yes, there were numerous incidents of personal violence and robberies running up to Christmas. In the damp lethargy of the new year, things quietened down for a month or two.

And then, beginning maybe three or four weeks later, there was a whole lot more. Some called it 'gang-related'. Others insisted it be called 'group-related', arguing that a certain glorification comes with the word 'gang'. Young people were consulted. They were canvassed and interviewed. Local councillors, MPs and youth workers debated the terminology. Nobody knew for certain how many people were involved in the robberies, muggings and attacks. Some reported six and sometimes there were as few as two or as many as ten. Others yet said it was both boys and girls. But the big three – Lester, Ommie and Carl – they were something else entirely. They were supreme. A hydra. A triumvirate of Moriartys. They carried knives, bicycle chains and baseball bats. Used bricks, their fists, CS gas, anything they could get their hands on: an iron, a hammer, axe handles, *axes*, debris from building sites. They didn't talk, usually, unless to threaten or instruct you. They wore hoods – *hoods*, not 'hoodies' like a baby might wear in its buggy. They had their own language. They didn't have a home. They were a couple years older than me at best. And this was them:

On 17 April, around 9p.m., they kicked in the garden door of 33b Carshalton Road, catching the Davies at dinner. The Davies, newlyweds, 23 and 26, with an eighteen-month-old baby girl, were just starting a takeaway curry. The husband's face looks like a naan when his photo appears in the papers. Browned, swollen and lumpy. Torn and chewed. They keep kicking him after he's blacked out. And they have a go at his wife. There were rumours of an abortion. It could have been any of the three.

On 24 April, Ashley Taylor, 14, was shot dead in the bath. He'd been excused from school because of a heavy cough. Doctors pulled eight bullets from his arms, neck, chest and legs. Ashley's classmates lay poems and flowers outside the council block where his family lived. They painted a mural at the youth centre and made the video collage in his memory that you can still see on YouTube today. His girlfriend left a long stem red rose with a card that read: 'I miss you like air you'll never be forgot in my heart. Mabey c u on d oderside. Ashley I ceep epxting you to txt.' Ashley's uncle, the family spokesman, vigorously denied his nephew ran with any gang. Nobody believed him. Not a one.

On 3 May, around 3a.m., they stormed into Charles Kikwete's flat, a ground floor maisonette that, it was reported, 'He kept immaculate despite having the use of only one hand'. They take £80, his keys, mobile phone, Oyster card, and iPod. And his false hand. A joke to them, but there are police everywhere, a helicopter and sniffer dogs. Nobody could find the hand, despite the £2,000 reward put up by the office block where Charles worked nights cleaning. Charles was 51 and reported hearing multiple voices before blacking out. He never saw who broke his sternum, collarbone, nose and three fingers of his only hand.

On 11 May, at around 10p.m., Kelly Johnson returned home from collecting her 12-year-old daughter from a birthday party. The Harvester or somewhere. Kelly's husband is in the Medical Corps in Iraq and isn't due home for another three or four months. Her body, charred from the waist up, is found bent face down over the bed rail and tied with electrical cords and the stockings she'd been wearing. Kelly's daughter sees boys in hooded tops, and locks herself in the toilet. She makes it out the window, only to fall two storeys and break both knees. The police chain a Witness Appeal sign to the lamp post on the corner. A black bandana is found in the bedroom. And there is the DNA evidence, too.

Just which of these attacks – and there were more, on the street and on the buses, on the trains, outside schools and in people's cars – just which of these attacks could be attributed to Lester, Ommie and Carl couldn't have been at all clear to M—. Even the police and the press didn't immediately link the crimes to any specific group. There were a handful of local street gangs. And new ones fighting to establish themselves all the time. It was only later that we saw it must have been LOCK Crazy Crew who had terrorised everyone for so long.

What I mean is it was only after they were gone that those things stopped happening.

At least the worst of them did.

M— saw to that. He saw to it, however accidentally, that there was a certain hope breathing in us – a hope that grew, you have to believe, in proportion to his isolation and misery. He didn't want notoriety. He didn't want to be in the news, a celebrity of sorts.

He wanted Tara and his parents back.

He wanted the impossible.

And he must have known the impossibility of it, too.

In the end, I think all he wanted was to settle the score. What he did along the way … well, I think he wanted to tell me. After I broke into his house for him, we started seeing each other more frequently, sometimes even at his doing. But, apart from telling me about his eyeflash, he never said much. He never admitted anything. He kept his counsel.

Look, I know it's a cliché, but silence speaks volumes. Ask anyone. Or try this: *hint* that you know something. Put it about subtly and let people believe – don't say anything definite – but let people believe you know something. Could be whatever. When they don't start quizzing you, when they don't challenge or correct you, well, then you know they think you know what you're on about.

I didn't know it was M— in the news for a long while. I didn't see how it could be. I had my suspicions, but it was only later that I knew for certain.

Exactly the same for M—. I don't think he knew who, for pennies, slaughtered everyone he loved. How could he? CCTV wasn't any help. It showed three hooded figures heading up the high street, away from his house after the break-in. The figures aren't together. First two are maybe 30 metres apart, one walking purposefully, like he's intent on making a train, and the other *rolling* in such an exaggerated fashion that he looks … well, it looks false, like something out of a cartoon show. (For who, you wondered. For who and for why?) The last one's running, absolutely pelting it. There is something about the way he runs that tells you he's young. The athleticism? The raw urgency? I don't know. He just looks it: young.

I've got no way of knowing what M— saw when he opened his front door and got cracked with the baseball bat. He told the police he didn't see anything. But I bet he did. I bet he did. I think he saw them. Or at least remembers them later. Remembers something that he keeps to himself – but then in a way shares with the world, given everything he ended up doing.

If he didn't remember whatever it was – their build, their eyes, a scar, a piece of clothing; their gargoyle lips, their gargoyle teeth, their gums when they grinned – I can't imagine how he could have started the hunt. You?

It was late May when the press got wind of M. Not M—, if you follow, not my neighbour and friend. But M the mystery, M the hero. M: *The Story*. While they had covered the local crimes – covering their varied and disparate angles, everything from 'white flight', to the effect on house prices, to interviews with spouses, siblings and parents of the dead, with community activists, old Rastas and local crusties, footballers and pop stars who had grown up in the area, those young people who sounded almost gratified to blame the press for portraying them negatively and as violent – there was nothing concrete about the intervention of a passing stranger, about the person who appeared and vanished without a word and who nobody could describe.

Nobody.

Witnesses, victims and culprits alike doubted their recollections, doubted they'd seen anyone at all. 'Once seen, never remembered' and all that. At first they thought they'd seen someone, but when they looked around he was gone.

If there was anything in the press it was only one or two lines buried somewhere in the middle of the story. *The unidentified stranger who ... The Good Samaritan ... Police would like to speak with the person seen ... is believed to have survived thanks to a member of the public who ...* Couple weeks of that and you could see something was cooking, something was happening, that there was a story here. Goose pimples right up your arm.

Press went apeshit.

News became news and, next thing you knew, there were TV crews on the high street, at the train station, outside people's homes, interviewing witnesses, long-term residents, young professionals who'd seen investment potential in the area, shopkeepers, head teachers, and charity workers. One philosophical old lefty with the sort of specs and pointy beard you only ever see on someone shaking a collection tin outside the library speculated M was the physical embodiment of the socialist spirit, in that 'His mission is to deliberately thwart the soured consumerism that predicates and poisons the lives of everyday people.' A few young people, on camera but backlit, their voices over-dubbed by some jobbing Footlights pro, insisted they knew the identity of the hero, that he was one of their peer group, but wouldn't be persuaded to give up his name. 'Nah, man, nah,' they'd say, and dismiss the reporter with a wave. 'Nah, man. He one of us. He one of us. I ain't no snitch or nuffink.' The owner of the local health food shop said that 'This heroic individual' could in fact be a ghost, a 'wandering spirit', I remember him putting it. Church officials dismissed this with a chuckle, telling us it was Christ's message to love thy neighbour and – wouldn't you know – that happened to be the subject of their sermon that coming Sunday! Police spokesmen warned us against vigilantism, while reminding us that many of the deeds done by the 'person or persons unknown' were 'simple acts of civility', something they themselves had been working on via the Yo Respect! programme and its outreach into schools.

The police had a point. While M had stopped a midnight mugging, tripped up a purse snatch, thwarted an armed robbery, ended a gang initiation (a beating), pulled a drunk from a bin fire, and spooked a carjack, most of what he did in those early days was only heroic if you think about how willing we are to look the other way when we see something happening. How quiet we are when something needs to be said. Stats prove it. Around two in every three Germans take a stand. More than half the Spanish and the Italians do. Even the French. *The French.* Us? Not even a third. And the numbers shrink every day.

But M:

He scared off a flasher at the playground.

He returned a dropped wallet and two mobile phones.

He directed a distressed mother to her lost child.

He guarded the schoolgirl being offered a ride home by some man.

He held a compress to the woman knocked down in a hit and run.

Stepping from the shadows, he chased off neo-Nazis carving a swastika into the turf in the hilltop park.

… And nobody could tell you what he looked like? Nobody (nobody but me) could tell you if he was blonde or a ginger, a chav, a tie-wearing bean-counter, heavyset or thin, the colour of his eyes, the colour of his hair, the sound of his voice, what he smelled like, the pallor or brown of his skin? *How*? Who was he? Why did he do it – why did he do *any* of it? Where did he come from? For at least a week, everyone speculated he must be homeless, the sort of someone who you never notice and who is likely enough to be on the street all hours day and night. We scrutinised the homeless in the parks and on doorsteps, outside the hostels and B&Bs …

Nothing.

About all anyone was prepared to swear to was that he was a he. That they'd seen him – but when they looked again he'd disappeared.

The press didn't like it. Or really, they loved it to bits but wanted more. Which is how the competition came about. One of the local papers came up with it. They said all heroes need a name. They said all heroes *deserve* a name, and that our hero deserved one no less than Monty, than Churchill, than …

I must have come up with two dozen ideas before I landed on the design I'd show to M—.

six

I've got a theory about M, about why everyone took to him faster than a flame. It's because we don't believe in God any more, but still want to feel protected. I won't go as far to say we feel a *yearning* for God. That would be wrong. That would mean there is a God but he's gone walkabout. Bunked off. We realise there is no God, but something in our bones makes us want to believe we're being looked after. M struck that chord. He hit for six. He made people feel safe, made us feel like we mattered. Like you don't have be on guard when you're on the bus home or off to the shops. He didn't mean to, but he did it all the same. People felt watched over. We felt protected.

If I believe in anything, I believe in M.

The second time M— saved me I was in the hilltop park twenty, maybe twenty-five minutes from home. I'd bought a Lucky Duck and a Luk B Wit U and won a fiver. Before that, I'd gone to see my probation officer, something I had to do three times a week. From where I was sat in the golden evening sun, you could see the great swell of the Gherkin, the Eiffel-like telecoms tower over Crystal Palace, the solid, straight shafts of Canary Wharf and, much nearer, the leisurely ripple of the rainbow-striped flag outside the Prince Regent. The pub's windows were frosted, which made it all the more alluring. I wanted in on its secrets. I wanted to see what went on inside. The liveliness, the music, the openness. Oh, and the people, too. But being tagged held me back. Being tagged, of course, meant I was on the Intensive Supervision and Surveillance Programme, or ISSP, that's all the rage these days. If I'd had the guts, the tag would've been easy enough to remove. I could have cut it, bashed it, wriggled out of it with a bit of cream, or just stretched it and stretched it until it would slip off like a sock. But I didn't do any of that. Didn't even try. Why? Because it terrified me. If I was caught without my tag, I'd go to jail where I'd be bent in two, beaten, and opened up like a glove puppet. And because I was tagged I couldn't chance it and pretend I was the four or five months older that I needed to be to go to the pub – not even try my luck at the offie for a tin or two. Being tagged put The Fear in me. It made me feel I was being watched, like the tag was linked to all of the tens of thousands of CCTV cameras, like they were watching *me*. Like God is supposed to do.

But I could sometimes forget about all of that when I was in the park. I didn't go there often, but some days I just had to get out and get away. No more mums. No more missing dads. No more sitting in my room with nothing to do, no more studying, probation appointments, scratchcards, tags, and no more being watched. There weren't any cameras in the park, nothing to remind me I was being scrutinised by some all-seeing eye. And unless there was dog poo or it smelled like wee, I always sat under the same tree, from where you could see the sky, the monuments glinting and blinking in the distance, the pub, and the footpath that curled into the nearby woods where men, it was rumoured, or maybe I'd read somewhere, would meet after dark.

But tonight it wouldn't be dark for a long while. It was one of those summer evenings when something about the laziness of the sun says it's not going anywhere. A sky so blue it was positively agonising. The grass must have been cut that afternoon: there was a sharp, almost reckless fragrance to the air, and the cuttings hadn't yet browned in the sun. I felt like sprawling out and running and spilling around and holding tightly onto something all at once, the way the air and the grass and the light and the open arms of the trees and the roll of the park all combined to form a single, powerful and scented sight that seemed to … it made me want to be kissed.

God, I ached with it, Stephen. *Ached with it.* I lay back, closed my eyes and pictured being kissed again. I remembered what it was like, how it felt, that first and only time. What I must have looked like – and what he did too. I won't tell you his name, but I will say that he was just as nervous as I was when, with this impulsive and quickening energy, we found each other's quivering faces and tensed bodies and, wrapped in each other's un-muscular arms, we kissed in the dark of the playing fields behind our school. It was the night following exams. We were released for the summer. He leant me against the tennis court fence and blushed when I brushed back his hair, which had a way of falling across his eyes. His hair just about broke my heart. We were hard in seconds and slick with sweat. I could feel him against my leg. And I knew he could feel me too. We touched. He said I tasted of cider. I licked my lips and told him he did of strawberry wine.

But after that night the boy ignored me. Then Dad left. I turned sixteen and Mum went mental. We had to move. A new house in a new street and new faces in a new school and no Dad and no happiness in Mum and not one friend. I hadn't been kissed since. Two long years.

It didn't look like it would happen tonight either. Nothing would happen. I could feel it; the feeling depressed me. There'd be nothing. Telly. Fish finger bap. The newspapers and maybe a peek online that would last hours before I knew it. Bed. A wank and the nagging guilt that always came after *I* came. It would be midsummer in two weeks, and soon after that, the longest day of the year. And then, if I kept out of trouble, they'd remove my tag. That wouldn't happen until September. September was ages away. A whole season. Waiting to be untagged made me restless. It made me angry. I was lonely. I needed to explain – to anyone – that I wasn't a bad person, that I wasn't dangerous. Explain and he would listen. Listen and see I wasn't a thug. Talking to him, I'd grow confident. He would tell me about himself, the things he did and the things he had hid and how he learned to stop hiding. He was brave and I'd be brave because of him. He'd teach me. He'd show me things, everything I ever need know to become the person I wanted to be. I closed my eyes tight and pictured how we would look at each other, the two of us talking for hours, relaxed, looking at one another like characters in films Mum and I liked to watch on rainy Saturday afternoons. *High Society, Love Actually, Born Yesterday* – that sort of thing. We would kiss and we would kiss and our fingertips would touch and –

'Nice evening,' the man said.

I jumped. *Wshh*: flat out straight to my feet. Banged into the tree like an oaf. I hadn't heard the man coming and now he stood before me, as though somehow sprung from the earth. He had the hair of a civil servant, stiff and sculpted. A small belly bulged bowl-like from under his black polo shirt. Hands on his hips sort of cheesily, like an explorer on the shores of a new land, he smiled at me. I don't know how long I'd been lying there, but I saw I'd been having the sort of thoughts that, let alone out in the open, could make me feel … criminal, if I'm honest. I felt guilty. Probably looked it, too.

'Yes, nice,' I said, adding stupidly, 'I was just lying there.' I think I actually pointed to the tree.

Why? Thing is I was compelled to prove I hadn't done anything wrong. That's what being tagged does to you. It turns something as innocuous as a greeting into an indictment.

Not knowing what else to say, I rubbed my elbow. It was grazed.

'Well, you're no acrobat,' the man said, and laughed. He had a dog lead over his shoulder, a silvery chain around his neck, and wore a wedding band. He looked about fifty, and smelled of musky soap. Something about the way he looked at me made me worry that I was covered in grass cuttings. I brushed myself off. He was maybe six or six-two, if you count his hair and all. No giant, but seemingly twice as big as me.

We were silent. It went on and on. So it was a relief when a noise reached us from over the crest of the hill. It was someone shouting.

Soon there was more.

For a moment, the man and I watched a pack of kids heading for the woods. They were boys about my age, play-fighting and pounding their chests. Some wore baseball caps and a few had hoods. Some had both; there had to have been seven or eight of them in all.

'Your mates?' the man asked. I could tell he was looking at me, but I was following the kids with my eyes.

I wanted to tell him no, tell him they'd probably kill me, tell him they didn't like people like me. But I couldn't say anything; you learn somewhere along the way not to go around telling strangers that you're …

I'd never told anyone. Not in words, at any rate. Every time I so much as thought about telling someone or practiced saying it, the words wilted on my tongue. Two words, five letters all in all. But nothing ever left my lips. Not a sound. Not about that. And so all I did was say something to the man about it getting late and having to get home. It was the last thing I wanted to do, but I found myself saying it all the same.

'Pity,' he said, 'to be stuck indoors on a night like this.' He gestured as though introducing me to the air. 'But I suppose you must have homework.' He paused before adding with a sympathetic smile, 'or is it revision?'

Before I could say anything, the man swung the lead from his shoulder and called for his dog, 'Mag-gie, Mag-gie.' He whistled three sharp notes and, when the dog didn't show, walked some distance off, going back the way I thought he must have arrived. He stopped at the crest of the hill, stood for a moment on the path, his hands on his hips, surveying. He shouted for his dog louder than before, '*Mag*-gie. *Mag*-gie. Maggie, Maggie, *Mag*-gie.' There was an urgency about his voice and he strode back down the slope, past me, calling and whistling for his dog. If there was anyone else around they didn't take any notice. I didn't see anyone and, anyway, I really don't think anyone would have cared. People are like that. People can be selfish and cruel.

But not me. I wanted to do something to help the man. Or, truth to tell, I wanted to do something to prove I wasn't a criminal. I figured if I helped a stranger find his missing dog … I felt the weight of my tag and, for a moment, felt guilty for wanting to benefit from someone else's sense of panic and loss. Sickened.

I started calling after the dog too. The woods where the hooded kids had gone were the opposite way I needed to go to get home before curfew. But I couldn't see where else the dog could have got to. I checked my mobile: I had thirty, thirty-five minutes. Cupping my hands around my mouth, I shouted for the dog. The man was maybe fifty metres away, near the boarded up lavs on the green that sloped down toward the pub. He was whistling and calling for his dog louder and louder. He sounded angry, upset, like he thought his dog – a floppy-eared spaniel with a liver-spotted coat, as I pictured her – was gone for good. I thought about all those news stories of dogs gone missing, how they're stolen for fights with pit bull terriers. A spaniel wouldn't last a minute in a dog fight. Like me in prison, it would be ripped to bits. The man must have been thinking the same thing, because he was heading at speed up the slope again, heading back the way he'd just come, as though wanting to marshal passers-by to join the search.

But there was nobody to help. Nobody but me. Jerking my thumb toward the trees, I indicated I'd check the woods. I gave the man a little smile, guessing how upset he must be.

The woods were quiet but for the smaller trees creaking in the breeze. I hurried along one of the squirrelling paths then down another and another, calling after the dog. There had to have been a dozen or more paths all going in different directions, hooking and re-latching back into each other. The dog could be anywhere. I felt sorry for it, picturing it lost and wet and sad and crying. And I felt bad for the man, having to return home without his dog, worrying all night. I kept calling and calling after it and trying to whistle like the man. My voice carried far, and I had a plan in case the hooded kids showed up: I'd engage them straight away. Make sure they saw I didn't think they stole the dog, and then get them to help out. 'Gratifying Empowerment' my probation officer would call it. But I didn't see the hooded kids. And I didn't see the dog. And I knew that I'd have to sprint all the way home if I didn't get a wiggle on. Checking the time on my mobile, I started back toward the edge of the wood.

'Anything?' the man asked when he caught me up. He sounded eager, like he was trying hard not to panic.

I told him I hadn't seen anything or anyone and started to say I was sorry but needed to go, when he held up his hand and hushed me quiet. We listened for a moment, peering all around us through the trees.

Nothing.

Not a sound.

I was as nervous for the dog as I was for the man. But when I felt his hand on my shoulder, I was nervous for me. We were off the main trail, surrounded by bushes and trees.

'I'm no *poof*,' he told me.

I couldn't speak. Couldn't even nod. I thought if I could just keep looking like I was looking for his dog, then everything would be all right. The man would see I was trustworthy, that I was kind. He'd let me be.

But what he did is circle behind me, holding me by the shoulder. I knew I should circle right along with him, keep him in sight – or not even look but just kick him and run. But if I did anything like that – anything *at all* like that – the police would come after me and would see I was tagged and I'd be sent to prison, where the other prisoners would do things to me while the guards looked the other way.

So what do I do but keep looking for the spaniel to come bounding through the bushes. I keep looking for the spaniel or the gang of hooded kids. I'd waited a long time and I'd looked everywhere for a kiss, but I don't think I've looked for anything harder my whole life than for that spaniel or those kids.

When the man pulled the dog lead around my neck and yanked me to my knees I knew it was over.

'You *poof*,' he hissed, pushing himself against me and twisting the lead tight.

Those are trees, these are woods, that is a bird: that's exactly what I see, exactly what I think. I can barely breathe; my throat is dry and my eyes are moist and the man starts rubbing himself against me, here, on the back of my head. *These are trees, those are birds* … I start gagging. I vomit, but have to swallow it. I think it will only make the man angry. I want to spare him that: I want to spare him from getting angry.

'*You cocksucker. You* filthy *cocksucker.* You think I don't know what you want, lying beneath that tree.'

There is the clank of his belt, the zip of his fly.

That was a bird, these are trees and that … and that …

His hand keeps hitting the back of my head as he tells me what he's going to do. He tells me he has something for me. He tells me he isn't a poof. He *assures* me.

'You're a bitch. My bitch!' He kicks my feet apart. 'What's this? Little bitch got a little bitch tag? Bitches don't wear trousers, now do they?' Then he says in what he thinks must be a coaxing voice, 'Got something for you.' Then he punches me in the ear. Grabs my head and tells me if I don't start sucking him off – he'll count to ten – he'll tell the police I attacked him in the woods. He says I'll go to jail. He's right. I think I'd better do what he tells me. I don't and he'll kill me.

He's standing right there.

Some time later – I forget when exactly – the man's name appeared in the paper. I never saw his photo, not until much later, when they showed it on telly. But that's hardly the point. The point is he went missing. Gone. Last seen the day I saw him.

I didn't know the missing person and the man in the woods were one and the same. Not at first.

And I promise you I never saw his photograph until much-much later. Only the news story, in print. I didn't have any time for it. I mean I figured it was just about another man who, like Dad, must have run off, left his wife, his kids, his job, his home … everything. So you can bet I didn't feel sorry for him. And couldn't be fucked to read up on it either.

But I still think I should have said something to the police. I should have reported the attack. I should have made sure he didn't attack anyone else. I didn't. I never said a thing. It's not shame. Not exactly. More because M— told me the man wouldn't hurt anyone again. He told me he'd sorted it.

And, Stephen? Stephen, I really did think he must still be alive.

seven

What M— was doing in the park, at that hour, on that particular evening, I didn't know. I didn't figure it out straight away. Not until some time had passed – and long-long after he told me when I saw him late that same night. He said he'd been out for a walk, just having a walk and a think.

He said, 'It helps me think,' … two, three, four, five, then: 'walking.'

But, you ask me, he was following the hooded kids – or was engineering some method by which they would find him. I've got no way of knowing for certain, but I think M— was lying in wait for them. Waiting to see if they were *them*. But when the kids don't do anything, when they don't take the bait … well, I do. I would have swallowed it whole too, if M— hadn't given up the trail and saved me.

There weren't any benches in the wood. There wasn't anywhere to sit down, where M— would have looked like he wasn't doing anything other than enjoying a summer evening (and, inside, mourning for his parents and Tara, like he had all but told me he'd been doing). He said he'd been out having a think; I can only think he'd been thinking about his family. So, with nowhere to sit and think, he found himself wandering around the looping, earthen paths through the trees.

And earlier, when he first saw the hooded kids, I imagine, he'd just been kicking about. Like me, before I plonked down under the tree. But then the kids started shouting, stabbing the air with gun-shaped fingers, leaping up, swinging their fists – BAM! – hammering their chests and, jostling for hierarchy in their pack, hooting like young apes. M—, from wherever he is, sees where they're heading. He circles into the woods ahead of them, inviting the confrontation, trying to appear vulnerable, like a victim, hoping they will be *them*. He doesn't look anything more than your average office worker out for an evening stroll, mulling over everything going right or wrong with the job, with the family, the car, wondering if it's going to be another takeaway pizza tonight or …

M—'s ordinariness is his cover. His ordinary ordinariness. That and his apparent preoccupation. He walks absently, like he has something on his mind, stopping to think here and again, kicking the pebbles at his feet or looking up at the trees, at the birds darting after evening insects. It's what detectives do on telly. They pause to stare into shop windows, to tighten their laces, fake a phone call. You make it look like something else is happening other than what you're doing or intending to do.

It's what M— must have done.

It's what the man did to me.

There never was a missing dog.

I hate to think what M— thought when he found me. And I can only imagine what he was doing before he did. Having seen the kids heading for the woods, he would guess they were going somewhere to skin up. If it was him readying a spliff, he would do it out of sight, somewhere where he wouldn't be seen. But he doesn't do drugs. He doesn't know the first thing about skunk or hash or whatever. Which is where he makes his mistake: the kids wouldn't care. They would crumble up their weed and smoke it out in the open. They don't give a toss. They know nobody will say a word. They're not scared of getting caught. Not like M— would be. But he can only guess their actions by referencing his own. He has to measure his actions then multiply everything times ten, square and distort it, he learns when he's in the woods, wandering about, guessing which way the kids went, which way they're coming, always listening for the sound of them speeding up from behind, always waiting for the eyeflash, the great bursts of light in the corners of his eyes that predicates him whipping superfast into action.

But the eyeflash doesn't come. The kids aren't in the woods. It's only a cut-through to wherever they're going. Home, a friend's, the chippie. And, all the time he's spent looking for them, all the time he's spent waiting for them to come at him with their hoods drawn tight and the rigid brims of their baseball caps pulled low, they're some distance away. The trail has gone cold.

In all, only a few minutes pass since he's circled around the woods. He feels empty, confused how he arrived here, by who he's become: an early middle-aged, middle-income IT geek, thin as the young trees, bewildered that he's here, wandering around the woods not long before nightfall and waiting – *hoping* – to be confronted by a feral and weed-wilded gang of kids who'd knife you as soon as say ''Sup'. I don't believe M— was in any way suicidal, only that he didn't care what happened to him if it meant he could avenge the murders of Tara and his parents. And if that meant he had to steer himself into the path of … No, he wasn't suicidal, but sometimes I have to wonder if he had a clue about what he was doing. What would he do when he found them? What could he possibly do? Him?

I didn't see what M— did when he found me. I didn't hear him coming and I don't think the man did either. I was crying. The man was hard, aiming his erection at my mouth, beating off, and yanking me at him by the dog lead. The scent of him. The peppery pong of his groin. I wanted to scream; I vomited again, a mouthful of bile that I couldn't swallow this time and that would have splattered the man's legs if I hadn't turned my face away. I'd shit myself, too. The man had made me pull down my trousers. (I'm going to tell it like it is, Stephen. Sorry, but I have to.) He made me play with myself. He made me say things, made me tell him where I wanted it, where I liked to take it. It got him hard. Playing with myself *I* got hard. And when I got hard, I shit myself. The man gagged. He slapped me. Slapped me, slapped me, slapped me until my face stung. He didn't tell me to, but I told him again all the things he'd told me to say before, saying them at the same time he was saying, above everything I was saying, that he wasn't queer.

47

I just wanted to get it over with. I wanted to get away, get home, get out of town, get lost and pretend it never happened. I thought he'd kill me if I didn't do what he wanted. *Two minutes*, I told myself. *Those are trees and there are birds in the trees and there will be trees and birds again in just two minutes and ...* and before the man could hit me again, I nodded and was just starting to ...

But right then the dog lead went slack. Slipped from my neck. I saw a pair of feet standing beside the man, a pair of legs, thin as scaffolding. When I tried raising my eyes up I saw black. It rushed through me. I fell down and down. I won't say there wasn't a moment when I thought that would be easiest, that I didn't feel a certain ... well, a certain *relief*, blacking out. It meant I wouldn't have to think. I wouldn't be conscious of what was happening, of what they were doing to me.

Yes: *they*. When I saw the other set of feet I thought it must be one of the man's friends. Someone he knew from the Interweb or somewhere. Someone coming to have a go at me too. Like there was a queue.

But it was M—. I wouldn't have known it was him if he hadn't brought me home. When I think hard about it, I sometimes convince myself I remember getting into a car. Colour? Make? Interior? Haven't a clue. And there's no saying my memory isn't false. I suppose there must have been a car and that it was a taxi or a minicab: M— didn't drive. All I can remember with any certainty is seeing those same shoes – light brown brogues that came to an almost winklepickerish point – as I'd seen in the woods, only now I saw them outside my front door. M— asked me for my keys. I somehow fished them from my pocket. I couldn't look at his face, only his shoes. Mum wasn't home (thank God) and as I raced upstairs for the shower I heard the church bells sounding at the top of our street.

M—, even if he didn't know it, had saved me twice that night. He got me home for curfew. It was nine.

What luck.

A word about luck. Or really, about my luck and about scratchcards. I was hooked. Couldn't keep away. The designs. The brightness. The colours. Their shine and promise and how they seemed filled with so much … so *much* promise. It was all I could do to keep it to twenty-one a week. It wasn't just what little money I had, but twenty-one is also seven times three. Three and seven are lucky numbers: third time's the charm and seven – everyone knows that one, something biblical. I bought more than twenty-one scratchcards a week and I worried I'd be over-dipping into my well of luck. Over-dip and you're done for. You always want a bit of luck on your side, a bit on the ready for when you really need it.

And you need some luck to win at scratchcards. I had my favourites – or rather there were those that felt luckier than others: Cash Cow, Diamond Life, Treasure Chest, Jackpot, Money Tree, Golden Fleece, Hat Trick, Loadsa' Cash, Silver Screen, Pot o'Gold, Rockefeller … I would mix and match. Never more than two of the same card in one day and never the same card two days in a row and, for that matter, never any card from the number five scratchcard dispenser. At least not after I first got started. I'd never won on a number five. It's anyone's guess why.

So yes. I had my lucky cards and I always used my lucky 50p piece to scratch. Lucky, not only because of its seven sides, but also because, by luck more than by chance I liked to think, it was in my pocket when I bought my first ever scratchcard, a Treasure Chest, and won £70. I cleaned my lucky 50p with Mr Muscle whenever it looked worn and as though its luck might be wearing off. I carried it with me everywhere for whenever I needed a fix. They sell scratchcards all over the map, but I had my lucky shop. I had my lucky shop – Nimrod's Corner News (it's a Starbucks now) – and I had all sorts of lucky rituals to observe if I wanted to up the odds of me winning. I always wanted to win, but, way I saw it, I didn't want to use up all of my luck at once. So, working on a luck expenditure/reserve theory – an unqualifiable and accommodating luck expenditure/reserve theory that I made up and manipulated according to my needs – I didn't observe all of my lucky rituals all at once. It depended on how low or lucky I was feeling. Or how badly I needed the money. Apart from what I got off Mum and what I nicked from her handbag, scratchcards were my only income.

The theory, though, went something like this:

I considered myself averagely lucky, a 50/50 sort of boy. Good and bad things happened to me with more or less equal frequency. I lost Dad, but still had Mum. We had to move house, but Mum rented a new one. I got arrested, but didn't go to jail. That sort of thing. So, if I needed to up the luck stakes a little, say if I had my heart set on a 100 Grand (big payout but low odds of winning), I needed to increase my luck to more than the usual 50/50. I wanted something like 80, maybe 85 per cent (I was never greedy enough to go for the full 100, thus blowing all my luck all at once and not having anything in reserve). So, when I went to the counter to buy scratchcards, I'd cross my index and middle fingers. Made it difficult to hand over the money, but basic stuff once you get the hang of it. I always paid with pound coins, always handed them to the cashier face up in a stack. If one had three lions on the back, it went on top. You never scratch your scratchcards in the shop. Always scratch from left to right, holding the scratchcard in the palm of your left hand and holding your lucky coin so that the whole of the Queen's face is covered by your thumb, with only the crown showing. Those were the easy ones. Some of them. My lucky rituals.

Sometimes, though, I figured I needed to dig deeper. Sometimes I'd time it so I arrived at the counter of Nimrod's in seven minutes on the nose. Sometimes I'd walk past the shop three times before going in, alternately crossing fingers on both my hands. If I felt luck was against me, that I was sub 50/50 for whatever reason, I'd take a completely new route, or revisit a long-since-last-used route to the shop. Replenish the lucky juices that way. Sometimes I'd try a new shop, figuring I was bound to have a bit of beginner's luck. And sometimes when I was already in the shop and if I really wanted to go for it, I'd count to 210 (three times seven times ten), pretending I was busy deciding which drink or magazine I wanted, when all I was really there for was a scratchcard. Sometimes I switched my count to 30, 70 or 100, lengths of time that didn't seem as lucky as 210, but would mean I wasn't using up all my luck in one go.

I worried about that. A lot. You run out of luck and you don't know *what* will happen. Everything's left to chance. I'd be done for. I'd be dead. I'd be trapped at home forever. Mum would really bottle it this time and we'd lose the house. Or I'd do something stupid and get banged up.

Win at scratchcards, I figured, and I didn't have to worry about any of that ever again.

But only if I won big. Won big, you see, without trying anything *but* my luck.

Scratchcards were a way of toeing the water. And, in that way, not entirely different than my studies, trying this and that to see what came off for me, where I fit in, what I was good at, where I had a bit of luck. Design was hard work. But if you know a thing or two about words and don't mind spending half your hours alone with only words for company, journalism's a breeze. Ever hear the one about the lazy journalist? Well so did he: the joke was someone else's, he just reported it.

Scratchcards were like that. A way to achieve something without really trying. They were a way out, just so long as you had some luck.

Call me crazy, but when I was showering after M— rescued me in the woods, I figured I must have some extra good luck coming my way. Probably already here. Like my well of luck got deeper and wider, an extra chamber of luck opening up and already swelling with fortified extra lucky luck. Like I couldn't over-dip even if I tried. That's what I told myself. Hand on heart, it's what I thought as I soaped and scrubbed and soaped and scrubbed and washed my teeth without once looking in the mirror.

It was luck M— was in the woods.

I was lucky to live next door to him.

It was by luck we knew each other at all.

What the man did to me in the woods – what he did to me and what I did to him – I didn't think about. I couldn't. I wouldn't let myself. But it was so bad, I remember telling myself so I didn't use Mum's leg razor to open up my wrists, it was so awful that I convinced myself I must have some extra good luck now as a consequence. Payback. How's *that* for displacement? How's *that* for kidding yourself? For every action there is an equal and opposite reaction, so the saying goes.

So it went with M—.

So it went with M— more than I could have guessed.

I didn't hear him leave after he brought me home. He was gone by the time I'd finished showering. And late that night I didn't hear him – not at first – when I went into the garden.

You might say that I was trying my luck, going outdoors long after curfew, going where the monitor might not pick up my tag's signal. It scared me. And I looked ridiculous, I'm sure. Wide-eyed and ghosted, my mouth tight as an envelope, my chin raised in a manner I probably thought looked defiant. Like an inchworm, I crept back and back in the garden. Step, stop, step, stop, step … dragging my tag and me out of the arc of the patio light and into the shadows. I was trying to face up to things, convince myself I was brave, undamaged. But really I was bricking it.

He's here. He's watching.

He's come for you. He's hiding.

No, he's gone.

No, he's here. Smell him? In the bushes with a knife. A hammer. He's angry.

One, two, three, four, five …

All the things I said to myself. Again and again. I counted two minutes. Then I counted two more. The breeze eased up. It was still. Quiet. I looked up at the stars; you could actually see a few: Ursa Major and Minor, Orion's Belt … the usual stuff. Looking at them (and consequently not looking at what was happening around me) I could breathe again. I rolled my neck and stretched my arms. The fence at the very back of the garden was only a few feet away. It was covered in honeysuckle and shadow, but I knew it was there. For luck I was going to touch it. I inched toward it, a step at a time. With every step I wanted to sprint back inside. The fence was the furthest I could go; to go that far would be all I could do. I raised my arm and, with my fingers, pushed away the honeysuckle. I eased into the shadows – my arm, my shoulder, my head, reaching deep to touch the rough surface of the wooden fence – when from behind I heard the creak of a gate.

I leapt. M— was at his side of the fence before I landed. He saw it was me and, for a moment, there was a look of guilt across his face. Or maybe it was surprise. Basically, he looked like he wasn't expecting anyone to be there.

He certainly couldn't have expected to see me.

I didn't expect to see him.

We were alone.

M— rubbed his eyes and I suddenly hoped Mum hadn't heard me go out. I hadn't told her what had happened in the park. Wasn't about to. She was asleep when I snuck past her room, downstairs, through the kitchen, and out into the garden for no reason other than I needed to see if I could. So I don't think she heard a thing.

What time it was, I can't remember. Two in the morning? Three? I'd been in my room pretty much the whole time since M— had brought me home. Mum came back minutes after I discovered M— was gone. He'd left my keys on the kitchen counter, near the kettle. I made a cup of tea that I couldn't drink, and made one for M— in case he came back. Both cups were still there, on the side, when I tiptoed through the kitchen door. Mum was steadfast when it came to me doing my own washing up; I was just as adamant now that she didn't find out what had happened the park. She did and I knew she'd blame me. She'd say it was my fault. That was the kind of thing she'd said before, at Christmas, which is how I ended up getting tagged.

We didn't talk about that. And we hadn't talked about things before, hardly at all, which is probably why everything exploded like it did.

If I'm honest (stay with me for a sec), I brought it on myself. Morning after Boxing Day and I was hungover. I was a wreck, in a right proper mood. Mum had had a rough go of things since Dad left. Really rough. Christmas was always the worst. I could tell Mum did what she could to not think about Dad. It was as if she thought she could compensate for or somehow fill the vacuum of his absence by making things into some sort of über-Christmas. One night she came home with bunting for the stairwell. Next, it was tinsel for the mantle, for the kitchen door. It wasn't as though we could afford it (not without sacrifice), but, over the next week or so, she bought a real tree, a wreath for the front door, fairy lights with multiple settings, presents for me, for herself, for 'the house'; expensive biscuits in snowflake-painted tins, mince pies (not just any mince pies: M&S mince pies), brandy butter, cashews, continental chocolates in shiny foil wrappers, clementines with their little green leaves still attached, little brass bells that tinkled when you opened the kitchen door, wine, cava, Baileys, a whole crateful of fresh vegetables, a turkey AND a ham. The house looked Christmassy. It was scented with food and pine – scents that seemed seasoned to an even greater richness whenever Mum unscrewed another bottle of wine. She would let me have the 'odd glass'; after she went to bed, I would always help myself to the 'even one' as well. She wanted to keep the illusion intact, to keep it wassailing along, as crisp and as clean as though it could, at the drop of a bauble, become the setting for any of the Christmas films we watched together, the two of us, silently wishing Dad was there to get the fireplace working. And she was after me more than ever to do my bit: take off my trainers at the front door, hang up my coat, clean the bath after showering. I wasn't to leave empty mugs on the kitchen table or in my room. She checked that I put the soap back in the soap dish, goaded me to take out the rubbish, to hoover, to wipe the bathroom mirror free of the toothpaste flecks that speckled its surface.

If anything drove her over the edge it was me leaving dirty dishes in the sink. Honestly, it drove her wild. She said it was thoughtless; I have to think I sometimes did it intentionally – or if not intentionally, with the understanding it would upset her. Sometimes I did it because I was bored. Sometimes I wanted to see what happened next. Sometimes I was in a rush to get back to my coursework. Sometimes I couldn't be fucked. Like Mum, I drank a lot that Christmas. Drank a little with her approval and drank a lot more in secret. So when she had a go at me about some dishes the morning after Boxing Day, I was in no mood to take it. I asked her why Dad left.

Truth be told I didn't ask her. I told her why: she was driving me mad, nagging and bullying me, just like she'd done to Dad.

Mum threw a plate on the floor. It smashed at my feet. 'It's because of you. He left because he has a *poof* for a son.' She said he was ashamed. And so was she.

I'd never said anything to either of them. But it's like when you hint you know something secret without actually saying anything. You keep a lid on it and everyone figures it out for themselves.

Rub is, sometimes they don't like you for it. Leave it to people to figure out whatever it is for themselves and it can swell into a whole flugelhorn of resentment.

'Look in the mirror,' she screamed. 'Aren't you ashamed?'

I was. I was to blame.

Mum went out. To the sales, I guess. Me? I went off my trolley. Drank everything in the house then lurched down to the Horse and Cart. I had arguments in my head. I got into something of a fight outside the pub (I lost). By the time the police pitched up, I'd urinated in a potted plant and toppled the fruit machine. I smashed a window. I threw a Zimmer frame at its owner. Threw empty pint glasses at him too. At everyone. The landlady sat on me until the police arrived. I was crying. I threatened to kill her. I told her how: about a dozen ways. I was serious. Mum was called to the station. She had to accompany me to court. She had to get me a solicitor: Legal Aid and all that. Everything I'd done was caught on CCTV. Even the things I didn't remember doing, like pulling down traffic signs and knocking over bollards. Using a bollard to smash up the grocer's fruit stand. Smashing wing mirrors and 'attempting' to steal a scooter.

The magistrate said I was troubled. He saw that I'd been in trouble before, for all the things I did when Dad left and Mum went mental and I couldn't find anyone to kiss: I stole things and didn't give them back. So when I did what I did then, on top of everything I did before, the magistrate said he had no choice but to make an example of me. Nine months on ISSP. And from Mum, when I got home that night after she'd collected me from the police station, I got about as close an apology as I ever would. She'd lost Dad and I had to think she didn't want to lose me too. She came to my room and stood beside my bed. I feigned sleep, but I think she knew I was awake. After a long while, she sat down next to me and smoothed my head.

I heard her say, 'It's all right now. You go to sleep.'

Mum left £20 on my chest of drawers. I spent it on scratchcards, mostly Squids O'Plentys and Luk B Wit U's and a herd of Cash Cows. I don't know what came over me, but I blew all the money in one go. Won £50. So I bought Mum some food to cook us for dinner. And I did the washing up for a week.

We haven't talked about it since, not really. I suppose the worst part is that I sometimes believed her – why Dad left. I knew Mum didn't approve (she grew up in Doncaster), that she didn't like it. And I know that Dad, if he suspected it, wouldn't have liked it either. Not one bit.

But I suppose he had a whole list of reasons why he left and why he stayed away. Dad and I: chip and block. All I wanted to do was leave home. Get out and do my own thing. And find someone to kiss.

I wasn't going anywhere though. Not after nine at night and not for nine months.

'But look,' I told M—, holding out my ankle. The tag shone darkly. 'I've sorted it. Never again. Not ever.'

We were either side of the garden fence. The night was still, but for the breeze. The air smelled like freshly turned soil: the air smelled like earth and, even with everything going all topsy-turvy like that, it was comforting. Not exactly the winds of change, but a sense that things were getting on with getting on. Like a sort of normality was settling in. Only the tag made me nervous: I didn't know what M— would make of it. I half-thought he might turn on me. Walk away. He hadn't asked me about it, but I wanted to tell him all the same.

So I did.

I wanted him to hear it from me. If he missed my tag when I broke into his house that once, then he certainly saw it in the woods. With all of the break-ins and attacks in the news, it meant more than my life that night for him to know that the local violence had nothing to do with me. I wanted him to know I was better than that. I didn't say as much, but I wanted him to know that if there was anyone in the world who I wanted to be like, it was him.

I like to think he could see I regretted what I'd done. No more of it. It wasn't me. I'd never do anything like it again. Looking at him – or really him looking at me and his eyeflash not lighting off, but assessing and somehow accepting me – I think he must have seen the whole story. Or at least remember my arrest. The local papers gave it an inch or two. I'd pleaded guilty, which is why I got tagged and not sent down to Feltham or Rochester or somewhere.

I'm not a thug.

I don't like hurting people or seeing people hurt.

Sometimes I don't even like touching people.

But M— I wanted to hold. I never did. And I never told him how much I wanted to. But perhaps he saw it? Perhaps he, with his magical eyes, saw it in *my* eyes? I couldn't tell him I wanted to hold him. I couldn't say how much I wanted to be held by him any more than I could tell him how much it meant to me that he even knew my name, that he spoke to me, and that I wanted, more than anything, to have the courage I figured he must have to hold up his beautiful face to the world and stare it down, while it feasted on his brittle heart.

Later – much later – I saw we weren't all that different. Or, at least, I saw there were things he couldn't say to me, too. It wasn't until sometime after the winner of the newspaper competition to name M was announced that he ever revealed anything to me about his eyeflash.

But that night in our darkened gardens, he didn't say much of anything. And all I could manage to say to him that sounded anywhere near bona fide was thank you. Everything else sounded made up, it sounded false.

How I'd been in the park to clear my head.

How the man had approached me.

How I'd been tricked into searching for a missing dog that never was.

It was only after I'd finished saying everything I had to say (even saying goodnight sounded wrong – and God knows I didn't want to say goodnight) that I realised why I was talking so much. I didn't want M— to see how damaged I was, how much the man had damaged me. That, if anything, was the falseness in everything I said: everything I didn't say.

But if I hadn't said something, if by luck and by chance I hadn't seen M—, I think I would have just stayed away, hid my embarrassment, how broken I was, my shame, by hiding the only thing that radiated with the sum of them.

Me.

M— must have seen that. He didn't miss a trick. I think he must have known why I was talking so much. He hardly said a word. Just let me get on with it. When I'd finished, all I can remember him saying is: 'You don't have to thank me. I wish none of it had ever happened. Are you certain you're all right?'

I lied and said I was.

M— told me he'd sorted things. He told me the man wouldn't do anything to me again. Not to me or to anyone. He told me I shouldn't be scared.

I like to think he wished the fence wasn't there between us. I could have torn it down with my hands.

Later, trying to fall asleep, I pictured M— on the other side of our bedroom wall doing exactly the same. Stiff and staring. Turning and hot. Twisting. Kicking. Wired by thought. Only he wouldn't be thinking about me. He'd be thinking about Tara and his parents.

I can't imagine they ever left his head.

He never left mine. I couldn't think about anyone else. Not about Mum, not even about Dad, whose absence was strangulating. Just M—, just M— and me. If he could rescue me in the woods like he had, he could always save me from next door.

He made me feel safe.

He kept me warm.

When I laid down next to him, he kept me warm. He was like a crackling hot bar in an electric fire. I laid down next to him, imagining him right the other side of the wall. I smoothed it and smoothed it. I lay awake for what felt like hours, the two of us there, side by side, caressing. And it was only in those moments before I finally fell asleep that night that I wondered what M— had been doing at his garden gate. Was he going somewhere, off into the copse? Or maybe he was just coming back? Was that why he had been so quiet? Why *be* quiet? Why be *so* quiet? Was he sneaking home? Where had he been? What was he hiding?

It was strange. He'd changed clothes since he'd brought me home. The night was warm. It was dry. And yet M— was wearing his long coat.

Why?

eight

The competition to name M was front page in the local paper. They said he was too modest to name himself and it was therefore the civic duty of the general public to do so for him. The competition was aimed at schoolchildren, I expect. But there was nothing saying it was exclusively for them. M— wasn't called M yet. He had no name. He was simply called 'our' or 'the' local have-a-go hero.

But M— was always M, so I don't see the point of calling him anything but.

It was June, I remember, a damp do-nothing Wednesday or Friday, when the competition hit the stands, with photographs of people who they proclaimed were 'Local Heroes and National Treasures': Charlie Chaplin, Pickles the dog, Robin Hood, Ian Wright, Shackleton, W.G. Grace, some Prime Minister or another, and Michael Caine. In the centre of these was a silhouetted figure with a question mark where his face should be. Caption: CAN YOU NAME OUR HERO? You did and you would walk away with a £500 cash prize, a one-year gym membership, and vouchers from the local sports shop, Two Ravens Booksellers, the stationers, haberdashers, and dry cleaners, the Indian and the Chinese. Inside twenty-four hours more than 800 people entered – and something like three times that before the deadline hit. If the paper had the technology, I'm sure it would have had some little device that played the theme song to *The Italian Job* when you turned to the competition rules on page three. Like those musical birthday cards you see at newsagents. I checked the paper's website to see if they had the music there. The site was under construction. So I just got to work straight away.

It's difficult to remember the exact date I came up with the idea, but I do know it was early one morning, before Mum's alarm clock sounded down the hall, with the sun already slanting through the blinds. I woke up with it. I'd already come up with something like two or three dozen names for M. I was on fire, obsessed. But, that morning, I knew for certain that the competition's cash prize was mine. Mine!

I was so confident that I treated myself to a Gatsby, a Bankroll and a Cash Cow. Won sixteen quid.

The more I thought about it, the more certain I was there'd be a job in it for me too. Proverbial icing on the cherry. All the competition asked was you name the superhero. A retired ad-man, working with the paper's editorial team, would draw up a shortlist and put it to a readers' vote. The winning entry would be announced in a week's time, along with a logo created by a local artist.

I did my own design. This would clinch it for me. A name for M, a logo designed so skilfully, with so much *je ne sais quoi*, that someone – the retired ad-man, the editor, some slick-suited marketing hotshot who had never read the paper before but just *happened* to pick it up on the train, at the airport, at hospital visiting an ailing aunt … I must have had as many scenarios as I had designs – that someone would see the raw talent in me and would shove a job my way. The £500 cash prize I'd use toward a deposit on a flat; with a job I could pay the rent. I'd be out of the house before my birthday. By the time I was eighteen, I'd have a place of my own. Nobody knew more about M than me. I followed the story in six or seven different papers, online, the telly – even the radio. I saved clippings, printed articles off the Interweb and wrote my own versions. When I had to brave it after everything in the woods and would sprint to the shops for scratchcards or papers, or when I was returning home from my probation meetings, I kept my mobile primed in case I saw M in action. Photographs, videos and all that. I probably came up with thirty names for M. But the one I woke up with I liked best. And I designed what wasn't so much a logo, but something miles more iconic: a *symbol.*

Because that's what he was, I wrote in support of my entry. M was symbolic of the civility and heroism in all of us. Maybe it's apropos of nothing, but have you ever wished and wished and wished for something and then when it happens you can't decide whether it's real or if you're imagining it? Sorry, it's not like I want to eat you out of house and home, but you don't have any biscuits, do you? Shortbread fingers or …?

On 17 June, Kevin Wallace, a 22-year-old father of three, was stabbed when he returned home from the cinema with his girlfriend, Thandie Burnett, 20. They'd been to see … well, I forget what. Some romcom, if I remember. Thandie goes three doors down to collect the kids from the sitter and Kevin races home for the loo. Police speculate he surprises the intruders. They knife him at the top of his stairs. Stab him something like once for every year he'd been alive. They take his car, £20, his mobile, his life, and his Xbox. Forensics found partial fingerprints on the telly and in the kitchen.

On 21 June, not long before 11p.m., a pizza delivery man, identified only as Abdulah, 42, was hauled off his moped in Abbington Close. There are no witnesses. The gang rob Abdulah of his money, two pizzas, and his mobile. Shatter the plastic visor of his helmet and stab him in the stomach and back. Abdulah lives, but leaves his job, saying he was moving his family back to Kandahar.

On 22 June, Michael Oslett, a four-year-old, cycled into the street. The child's plastic tricycle is crushed under the wheels of a reversing lorry some fifty or so metres from home, where he'd been playing in the garden when his mother nipped indoors to make a brew. The lorry driver reports the incident. Michael claims it was a monkey who'd whisked him from harm. Later, his fantastical story broken by the offer of a Cornetto Flake, Michael confesses it had been a man who'd saved him, whom he describes only as thin and tall.

M— was something like six-two, and thin as a whisper. There was also something homunculus about him: gangly arms, his narrow chest and tummy. Big eyes. Face that was ever so slightly muzzled. And the way he seemed to just swing away into crowds and disappear, as though brachiating through the forest. Like a monkey.

You're not supposed to say that kind of thing about certain people. Even for others, it's generally frowned upon. But there was definitely something monkey-like about M—. No question.

To be fair, I look like a dog.

And you have to think I must have looked especially doglike when I showed M— my entry for the superhero competition. Like I was dropping a ball at the feet of my master. The shortlist would be selected in three or four days and I'd spent all the hours I wasn't doing coursework or at probation meetings drafting and redrafting my design. I used up a whole sketchbook before things finally clicked. I was proud of what I came up with. It was masterful. It was simple – laughably simple. Justifiable, too.

It was genius.

God, was it ever. *Genius.*

But it wasn't anything until I showed it to M—. Not anything at all. I waited all day for him to arrive home, only giving up my watch when anxiety got the better of me and I rushed out – literally ran – to Nimrod's and bought a Luk B wit U, and two Goldmines. (I won £12 and bought Mum some chocolates, not only because I thought I'd get some good karma for the competition if I shared my winnings, but also because I wanted to give her something for the money I'd nicked from her handbag a few nights earlier.) Then I went straight next door, to M—'s. If I had a tail it would have been wagging wildly when I rang his buzzer.

A week later and all I wanted to do was hide. I didn't make the shortlist. I doubt I even came close. I tried to convince myself the judges must have something special in store for me. A job, an assignment, a desk. I expected a phone call. *Expected* it. My heart leapt whenever the post clunked through the letter box. I checked my emails two, three, probably four times hourly, more than three-quarters convinced the paper's editor or the retired ad-man's colleagues were desperate to get in touch but were held up because they were so overworked.

Which is where I'd save the day. I'd be the trusty young office boy, the plucky apprentice, like Jimmy Olsen. Oh, and I'd be fucking magnanimous about losing the competition. Easy, seeing how I'd won something immeasurably more precious. A new life. A start. Dignity. A pay cheque every month or cash in hand (whatever they liked, I didn't mind). And there'd probably be something in the paper about me, a warm-hearted piece. Not a feature exactly, but maybe two hundred words and a photograph. It's embarrassing to think about it now, but I even practiced what I'd say: 'It was the anonymous heroism that inspired me. It got me thinking that I counted – that I counted, *too*. No, I'm not the hero.' I'd deepen my voice. 'I'm not a hero at all. I'm someone with a job to do, an apprenticeship, and I'm going to make the best of this opportunity to … No, it's not me who's the hero. Our accolades go to the man who; who; who …'

In the end, I was simply ashamed. Broken. It wasn't so much that I lost the competition, that I didn't win the money, but how excited I'd been in front of M—. My certainty that he was dead impressed when I – tarting about like a complete Tadzio – showed him my design.

'I've nailed it,' I informed him, holding my shoulders back and grinning like a beagle.

M—, in his quiet, heartbreaking way, smiled at me. He smiled at my design, which he held in his hands. He even laughed. It was the sweetest sound, small, like something sizzling gently in a pan. There was genuine happiness in his face, a happiness I don't believe he'd felt in some time. Not since he found everyone dead.

I like to think he was proud of me.

We were in his sitting room. M— was in the stuffed armchair by the window, in a thin shard of sunlight, listening patiently and blinking, while I, unable to keep still, explained the meaning – the 'rationale', I think I said – behind the design.

'Nobody knows what he looks like, right?'

I could tell M— wanted to look at me, but all he did was stare at his shoes. Or maybe it was my design he was staring at? I only know for certain that, out of nowhere, he started to squirm. He tried to disguise it by crossing his legs.

'That's what makes him so great: he could be anyone. He's someone anyone might know. You can't change that. Or you can, really,' I said, getting ahead of myself, 'but that would take the mystery out of it.'

My design was centred on a sheet of printer paper, hand-drawn in black ink with straight lines, squared edges, and done in a way to convey a variety of textures. There was the flat black background, filled with a large, smooth black star. Inside the star was the letter U; once recreated in textile it would only be apparent if you saw it from a tight angle. To the naked eye, to the passing stranger, the black U and black star would be practically invisible against the flat black background.

'It represents the superhero's ability to blend in, his anonymity.' My eyes started tearing up (I suddenly felt so noble) when I said, 'It also protects his need for privacy.'

M— nodded. Or at least it looked like he did. Just the once

'And the five points of the star represent each of the five postcodes where he's rescued someone or stopped a crime.' I listed the postcodes and some dozen or more of the deeds that were attributed to him. I didn't list all of them, but enough for M— to look at me with something like amusement and, later, I thought, a sort of mild horror.

And later yet, to my own horror, I realised M—'s sitting room looked the same as it must have always done. What I mean is it looked as though his parents were still living there, like they might walk in at any moment. It was their collection of framed photographs loading the sideboard. It was their stamped copper tray hanging on the wall. The photojournalism books were theirs, the slippers tucked neatly and within arm's reach beneath the sofa, the furniture itself; and the heavy floral curtains were drawn as they'd always been, to allow a narrow vein of a view of the front garden without giving passers-by chance to ogle everyone inside. But it was the tea service that really sent chills up my spine. It was set out before I showed up. Four cups, four saucers and enough biscuits to feed a family. A piping pot of tea. M— didn't touch the biscuits, not a one. He didn't sit on the sofa either, as though it was reserved and would, any minute, be filled by his parents when they came back from the shops, in from the kitchen, back from seeing off relatives at the airport or greeting guests at the front door.

'And the U?' I said. 'The U stands for U: text-speak, you know, for 'you'. And it also stands for 'Us'. That's his message: "We're in this together," he says by doing whatever he's done and then disappearing. "Forget about me: *I'm* not important. *We* are though. Collectively, we're important. As a community, a society. We're an Us and you," I made a u-shape with my hand, which I just about managed to hold steady, "U count, too."'

'That's very … comprehensive,' M— said, marvelling, I worried, more over my hammy performance than the design. He rested it on his knees and smoothed it with his hands (I almost passed out here). 'Very-very good.'

He studied the design for a long while. I beamed. M— appeared moved, touched in a way. 'Compelling,' he said and, after another minute or more had passed, 'Can you submit it by email? I'll scan it and send it in for you.'

Before I could say anything, he added, 'If you like.'

I did.

'Just a minute,' M— said and, asking for my email address, disappeared upstairs. I listened to see where he went, to know for certain if his room was adjacent to mine. But as soon as he was out of sight he didn't make a sound. You couldn't hear the scanner, you couldn't hear him type, or even his footsteps or the shutting of a door. Nothing. Not a thing. The only way I knew for certain that he didn't simply go upstairs and slump against the wall for a good few minutes is that when I got home there was an email from him in my inbox.

'This one gets my vote,' he wrote, and signed his name, M—. The scanned logo was attached. A jpeg. I still have the email – even today. And, much as it breaks my heart, I also still have the newspaper clipping of the competition winner, David Langdon, 11.

David, like me, had also submitted a design. His was a coat of arms with a lion nestling a dove, crossed behind by a sword and mace and done in what the paper called an 'urban style' (it looked like spray paint). His design was printed alongside a slick version rendered by the local artist, based on David's logo for M, whom he called the South London – or SoLo – Knight.

I barely got out of bed for days.

It's only over time that I managed to let that one go. And it's only with distance that I've been able to gain some understanding of what M— meant to me and of who I was when we knew each other, why I was too ashamed to see him after I lost the competition and how he shaped me. Looking back now, I realise I hardly knew who I was. I had some rounded idea of who I wanted to become, of course. A conception as aspirational as it was farcical and romantic. But how I managed to hang all of this on M— is something of a puzzle.

I adored him.

Stephen, I loved him.

He was a mystery. But perhaps that's love's reason in and of itself? He could be anything I wanted him to be and everything I wanted to become.

The perfect package.

After losing the competition, I kept to myself. It was a struggle, but I managed to not think how disgusting and sodden I must look to M— because of everything that happened in the woods. What he saw. But that didn't stop me from feeling as empty as the moon. I was lost. A loser. It killed me not to see M—. I suppose it was just as well that I was tagged and could go hours and hours, even days, without venturing out or saying anything to anyone. About all I did was stay in my room, only running out when I needed a scratchcard fix and to keep appointments with my probation officer, Darrell Thomas.

Darrell. I haven't told you much about Darrell. He was pushing 40, only a year or two older than Mum, and not much taller than me. He had thin dreadlocks down to his shoulders, a massive

Arsenal tattoo on his upper arm; and above his cologne you could smell the Superkings he was always smoking in the car park or, when it rained, out of his office window. The smoke clung to his hair; he had masses of it. Darrell doesn't come into this story much. He tended to treat our meetings as formalities, as though he knew from the word go I'd come good in the end. He asked me about my coursework, how things were at home, if I was looking for a job (I wasn't, not unless scratching scratchcards counts as seeking employment). I only mention Darrell now because I can see how it might not have been M— on whom I obsessed, but him. He was kindly. Supportive. And I certainly saw him more often than I saw M—. Darrell was caring … and I suppose it's worth saying he's black. I mean, for what it's worth, that's the truth. He wasn't one of these middle class whites trying to pass himself off as a Rasta after six weeks of drumming lessons in Mali or Melbourne or somewhere. Darrell had light black skin with freckles across his nose, two mobile phones, and an almost biblical way of speaking whenever he felt I needed a talking to or he was simply in the mood to lecture. There was a muscled yet playful physicality about him that I must have somehow picked up. I see it in me today. What I mean is the way I sometimes phrase things is the same as Darrell. He liked to flex his vernacular perspicacity as often as he would the muscles in his tattooed arm.

I suppose I was looking for someone on whom to model myself.

Oh, but M—, Stephen. Marvellous, mysterious, magnetic, monkish, monkey-like M—. I say that I saw less of him than Darrell and, in a way, that's true. But then I also saw M— everywhere. I hadn't yet twigged it that he was one and the same as M, the public hero (I never could and still won't bring myself to call him SoLo Knight), but I was following him all the time. I saw him every day.

Even when I was too self-pitying to go next door.

On 24 June, Rabbi Martin Fuglewitz, 57, was walking home from dinner at a friend's. It's midnight; he is attacked from behind, beaten to the ground, taunted. Anti-Semitic stuff. Kicked in the balls, his ribs, his head. Before he passes out, he hears the sound of something heavy hitting a tree, sees a pair of pointy leather shoes – but only for second. He said he didn't trust himself to guess their size or make. Whoever it was who saved him used the rabbi's phone to ring 999. The phone is found inside his jacket pocket. There is blood on the tree and on the pavement. And there were also bloodstained threads from what police believed to be the assailant's hooded top.

On 26 June, at around 10:30p.m., Sally Young, 37, was out jogging when she is dragged into a building site. Though weary from running most of her eight mile circuit, she fights back at her attacker – white, 25-35, between 5'8"- 5'11", and wearing a dark green hooded top – until he punches her unconscious. Sally wakes as the paramedics wheel her toward the ambulance. She sees detectives removing a pair of work boots and a sack-like scrap of cloth from a skip. The attacker was David Jameson, an out of work scaffolder, reported to police six days later by his wife. She'd grown suspicious after seeing the attack on the news and noticing her husband had replaced his new boots. His torn top – its hood proved to be what Sally saw detectives recovering from the skip – was found in the boot of his car. David got three years. He couldn't say anything about who'd knocked him unconscious, torn off his hood and stripped him of his shoes.

On 28 & 30 June, the mothers of two youths and the grandmother of a third reported an oddity. They went to the press and to the police. The press take up the story when they see the police are involved. The police get involved when they hear the press has been tipped off. Together they discover the event dates back some two weeks, to 16 June, to the night the three kids were out until long after midnight. The hoods of their sports tops had been removed: two were torn straight from the stitching and one was sliced cleanly away in one long stroke. All three kids were taken into custody on suspicion of being involved in the fight on the 122 bus that left one of their classmates dead. Knifed in the neck with a pair of scissors.

Next week and you couldn't miss it. Not even if you tried. Two dozen incidents, probably more. Kids with their hoods torn off – torn or sliced. Police and school officials were quick to label it a new trend in bullying. Flyers were distributed by local youth centres. Campaigners appeared on TV and in the papers. Young people were encouraged to come forward to give statements. They were offered protection and given amnesty. Although sheaves of statements were taken, the police couldn't gather enough information to confirm what everyone thought: pretty much all the young people had been engaged in some act of violence or anti-social behaviour just prior to their hoods being forcibly removed – so didn't they get what they deserved?

On 1 July, police raided M—'s house before dawn. He was taken into custody. I didn't see him for ten days.

nine

It's not something that deserves congratulations, and it's certainly not something I ever mentioned to M—, but the whole time the police held him at Paddington Green, I watered his garden at sunset. The cops guarding the front of his house, and the paper-suited forensic teams beavering away inside, meant I couldn't do more. Only stand there, in the evening, with my hose, arching its fine spray over the fence. It was all I could do to make things look alive for when he came home. He'd lost enough as it was. And God knows I couldn't sleep at all: M—'s arrest was all over the news. I begged Mum not to give an interview to the reporters who turned up at our door. But she did – though at least she did it anonymously: 'Local resident says', 'A neighbour reports' … that sort of thing.

When you think about it, it was a very M— thing to do. Everything he did, he did in secret, without recognition nor request. Same with me watering M—'s garden behind his back. I imagined every drop that fell would somehow absolve him, help prove his innocence.

Ha! Just who's the *real* innocent?

I wanted to rescue him. I thought I could too.

If that's not love, Stephen, I don't know what is.

Sometimes I have to think that if it hadn't been M— who got arrested, I would have missed the story completely. I mean it could have been just another nameless dupe groomed by extremists. Another someone to be wary of, avoid, suspect and ostracise. Another suspect banged-up for 28 days or however long, without charge.

Yes, M— was taken into custody for intent to cause terrorist acts. Him! M—!

At first I thought he'd been arrested in connection with the murders next door. It's only natural for the police to suspect a family member – I remember Googling it and something like two-thirds of murders are committed by someone known to the victims –but then why the dawn raid? Why the armed police? Why the white tent billowing stiffly outside the front door and forensic scientists in goggles and masks? Sniffer dogs.

No, this was something else. Something with *weight*. Five in the morning – BAM! Wood and glass everywhere. Thuds up the stairs. Room to room. Shouting. 'DOWN! GET DOWN! STAY DOWN! HANDS! HANDS!' Then M— in his striped pyjamas, handcuffed, head forcibly ducked, is tucked into the open door of the waiting police van. Flashing lights, the strain of the engine gunning like mad, sirens bouncing off the houses. Gone in seconds.

But for what?

Before the police could come round to see if we were all right or to take statements or whatever, I went to them. Breath like Ghandi's sandal. Crying like a florid fool. Barefoot and barely dressed and my tag on display. The pavement was cool, it was damp, but I went right up to the police and with a quavering voice and a million things to tell them, I said: 'He wouldn't hurt a fly. A fly! Anyone who knows him knows he wouldn't hurt a fly.'

And soon enough (or really, after a week, which couldn't have been soon enough for M—) the police knew it too. There's always this great debate about how long the authorities can hold and question someone on suspicion of terrorism. But what you don't hear so much (or what, if you're like me, you always forget as soon as you hear it) is how quickly they release some of the people they arrest. Mistaken identity. Bad information. Zero forensic evidence. Airtight alibi.

With M—, I have to guess it must've been some combination of all these things. Otherwise they wouldn't have let him go after only a quarter of the time they were legally allowed to hold him. They didn't find anything dodgy in his house, at his work, on his mobile. I can't imagine anyone having anything bad to say about him. But I don't think he had anyone who could vouch for him during the hours between … Whether he had ever purchased bulk containers of … If he had, on a set of dates, visited the … He'd lost everyone who could attest to what he did privately. M— was what the press called 'a loner' which is an indictment of a different sort.

It got right up my nose. I yelled at the telly when one of the channels (I'm sure you can guess which one) labelled M— 'a potential public threat'. I hit the telly. I kicked the couch. I pummelled my legs. Stephen, I punched myself in the face. *In the face.* Then I worried my tag was probably signalling to its monitor that I was losing it, both the plot and what little freedom I had. So, after that, I just cried. Cried and cried. Screamed – *God*, did I scream. Pressed myself against the wall between my bedroom and M—'s and tried to think of what to say, what I could do to let him know I'd help. That I knew he was innocent. That even if everyone else didn't believe in him, I did. I whispered to him through the wall, 'You have me. You have me. You have me, M—'

When I couldn't say it any more, when Mum banged on my door and told me to shut up, I raced out and bought a Silverscreen and a Hat Trick. Didn't win a thing, bugger all. I bought a £2 Money Puppy: no joy. An Aladdin's Lamp: nothing. So I got down to the one thing I knew I could do. Write. I gathered everything I knew about M—, everything there was online, on the telly, on the blogs, in the papers, in my head, and sat down to write.

After 2,000 words I packed it in. But I managed to knock it down to this, which is what I sent to the editor of our local paper:

'Let it be said that a man who knows no evil knows not himself, nor the soul of his fellow man.' If you don't know who said that, you needn't worry. It's not exactly Shakespeare, and it's not something handed down the ages from the Bible or the Koran or from Prime Ministers past. These words were spoken to me by Darrell Thomas, my probation officer.

I didn't get what he meant at first, but with the recent events in Stillman Terrace, I have gained greater understanding of what Darrell meant. Enough that I can offer this adjunct: *And look not at knowledge of evil as sin in and of itself, for it permits thee the ability to divine right from wrong, whether in thyself or thy fellow man.*

While the antiquated tone might make you feel funny, you're not alone. I think so too (and what a surprise it was to find myself composing those words). But I happen to know one man to whom this wisdom is no laughing matter. My neighbour, M—. While undoubtedly still recovering from the tragic deaths of his parents and girlfriend, he was arrested this week on suspicion of terrorism.

Let me say openly that M— not only knows the difference between right and wrong (and that he knows this with unimaginable intimacy, having found his loved ones murdered), but also that he only knows the evils of terrorism the same as all the rest of us do: as a potential target. He has no technical knowledge of weaponry (this I am certain will come to light), and he has no theo-fanatical ideology to justify any act of violence toward his fellow man. He is, in short, no different than you and me. I, with all my heart, look forward to the day he is free.

It can't come soon enough.

I made up Darrell's quote. The rest took me all night to knock into shape. At first, Darrell grumbled, even trying (unsuccessfully) to formulate some sort of worldly-sounding comeback. He was angry I hadn't shown him the letter before it was printed. But in the end, he didn't mind. He said it was good advice. He said it showed how much talent I had. He encouraged me, in his stentorian way, to enrol in another journalism course in the autumn, if not sooner. I offered to do a frame-able version for him to hang beside the sexual health and anti-knife posters on the wall beside his desk. I did and he did, too. And when M— returned home from Paddington Green, I brought over a copy of the paper. He'd been in prison for a week, and I hadn't seen him for at least three days before he'd been taken into custody.

If before I missed Dad more than anything, it was M— who, in those ten overstretched days, I missed more than … Imagine ten days without water. I was sickened. I felt raw. It was like losing your skin.

M— was a mystery to me. And yet I can't help but think how much we were the same. Or if not the same, I can see the strength of those things that, however fanciful it sounds, ran through the two of us like a thread. We weren't exactly *bound together*, but we shared … our isolation, which is, of course, something that by definition can't be shared. But … Look, I was housebound, on ISSP, fatherless, and confused by and ashamed of myself to the point of 24/7 sexual abstinence. M—, in police custody, he later told me, was only not alone when they interrogated him: twelve hours of sunless, baffling, cell-bound segregation; twelve hours of thumbscrew indictment and systematic, personalised examination, which is an isolation of a different sort: isolation by accusation. I imagine he had to have been literally and figuratively (and bewilderingly) stripped bare. And then – when the police realised their mistake, when they found nothing on his laptop, nothing on his mobile, no suspicious liquids or purchases, nothing in his bank account but for the timely paying of council tax, utility bills, and all but frugal withdrawals from the bank machines nearest his home and office – he was shipped back, with little more than a jargon-thinned and nearly anonymous apology, to his empty home.

It's true that there were relatives waiting to greet him: uncles and aunts and cousins and things. But they didn't stay long and nobody spoke to the press. I was embarrassed Mum had (she didn't say anything bad, but sort of left the door open). You ask me, and M— *sent* his relatives away, back to their homes. Told them to leave and right quick. I think he wanted to get back to work. To hunting down Lester, Ommie and Carl. I think he needed to. But he couldn't do it with everyone there, in his home, asking him why he was; what he was; where he was…

Yes, it was the tug toward and, rather conversely, the resisting of family that marked M—'s and my commonality. That's my theory. I can't say I understood enough about myself to have seen it then. But, like I say, it was only over time that I could overcome the ignominy of losing the competition to a child, and I have since developed some sense of self (and pride in myself, Stephen, for that matter). I can see it today. It was always there, always evident, however passively or mysteriously. I only hope M— saw it too.

I can picture M— with Tara and his parents. I can see how he'd be with them. His kindliness and his reticence, which measures not only his long-limbed love for them, but also, because of them, his vulnerability, which was mirrored physically in his spraddled and gangly self and in his hushed maniacal pursuit of LOCK Crazy Crew. He was a mystery to me, but I can see – and in some way must have seen even then – how he must have been the same with his parents. I can't imagine they'd have had any truck with him disappearing every nightfall. Hardly the sort of thing they'd approve of. Even if it was because of them that he was doing what he did. Their stark absence grew so copiously that they again had something approaching a physical presence. I can see how, throughout that spring and summer, he would have continued looking after them the best he could.

Picture it:

MOTHER (*Watching M— stir the casserole*): Not too much spice. Your father –

FATHER (*From the sitting room*): What's that about me?

(*Nobody replies, but M—, still at the hob, nods his head and continues to stir slowly. His father, coughing, lumbers into the kitchen.*)

What's that?

MOTHER: Where's your mug?

FATHER: Where I left it. Why is *he* cooking?

78

(*M— glances at the kitchen table, where he has already set out the glasses, plates and utensils for dinner.*)

Is nobody talking to me?

M—: Another five minutes.

MOTHER (*Feigning surprise*): That soon? You want it to simmer for at least an hour.

FATHER (*Still in the doorway*): You didn't use too much spice did you? (*To wife*) He didn't use too much spice, did he?

MOTHER: Where's your mug?

FATHER: I haven't finished with it yet.

MOTHER: If you bring it here I'll do you another cuppa. (*Pause*) I'll get it.

(*She begins to rise. M— glances out the window and sees it's getting dark.*)

M— (*Quickly*): We're almost ready.

FATHER: I don't *need* another. I'm happy with what I've got.

MOTHER: But it's cold by now.

FATHER: I hope he can cook. I'm starving.

MOTHER: Don't say such things. It's bad luck.

(*M— blows on a wooden spoonful of sauce before tasting it. He makes a face.*)

It needs more simmering.

FATHER: Listen to your mother. Or don't, I'm starving.

MOTHER (*Sitting down again*): There's no rush, dear. (*To husband*) Go back to your programme.

FATHER: What programme? I was asleep.

MOTHER: See? I told you it's cold.

FATHER: No it isn't. I finished it.

M—: We're ready.

(*Collecting the bowls from the table, he quickly spoons out the casserole.*)

FATHER: I hope he can cook. (*He leans over his bowl and smells the food.*) Mmmh.

MOTHER: Aren't you eating?

M—: I have to go.

FATHER (*Pausing before taking a mouthful*): What's the matter with it?

(*M— removes the bread from the oven, slices it, puts it in a bowl that he places in the centre of the table.*)

MOTHER: You need to eat. Sit!

FATHER: (*Chewing*) Good. Not too much spice.

MOTHER: Will you please sit down.

(*M— looks anxiously out the window. There is light still, but it's getting dark.*)

M— (*As though saddened*): I have to go.

MOTHER: Every evening! (*More softly, though with an accusatory note*) You weren't home when we had all that trouble. When they –

M—: What did they look like? (*He goes to the kitchen door and tests it's locked*). If you could just tell me what they … (*Now more to himself and slowly*) What did they look like? Were they tall? Did they say anything? What were their accents? Had you seen them before? At the shops or …?

FATHER: You should stay in tonight. Test match highlights are on at –

MOTHER: Oh, no they're not. (*To M—*) You need food.

M— (*Hesitating*): Maybe a bite.

MOTHER: We're watching Holby City.

FATHER (*Indicating M— with his fork*): He's not going to stay in for that now, is he? (*Shakes his head.*) You stay in and we'll watch the Test match highlights.

MOTHER: I don't like you going out every night.

M—: I can look after myself.

(*He eats a spoonful straight from the saucepan. Then another.*)

MOTHER: You can at least sit down to eat.

FATHER: You'll get hurt. All this crime. I don't like it. (*To wife*) And I don't like Holby-bloody-City either.

(*M— starts to reply to his father but stops. He leaves the kitchen and comes back a moment later, buttoning his coat. He watches his parents eating, and a smile spreads across his lips.*)

M—: I have to go.

M—'s family never struck me as religious. They had their traditions, I bet, but were they the sort who prayed before dinner?

I doubt it. I don't know the customs for that sort of thing. Or, if there are customs for that sort of thing, if M—'s family would have observed them. His father was probably older than his mum by ten years. M— was built like him. Or rather he was built like his father was built before he got older, less mobile, before he retired and grew a great big belly on his wife's cooking. Clarified butter and all that. It didn't supersize her. She was petite. In her youth, and going by the framed photos in the hall, she looked not wholly unlike Tara, what with her bewilderingly big eyes. M—'s mum had greying hair which she kept tied back in a ball and was quiet, guarded, as though she'd never quite come to live at ease here in her new country, and as though she was observing some custom from her homeland. Something that said, like others might say to a child, that it is better to be seen rather than heard, at least in public. But in their home it would have been different. Yes, M— was built like his father and as quiet as his mum. And I think he must have heard something from his parents – a scolding reminder from both – when under darkening skies and with nothing more lethal than his own laughably thin arms and whatever monstrous intent writhed away inside of him, he went back on the hunt.

I can't imagine he got any rest.

I certainly don't believe he had any peace.

He was out every night.

When I went next door to show him the letter I'd written in his defence, M— looked as though he'd only just arrived home. Or perhaps he was heading out? Yes, I think that's it. He was heading out for the night, helplessly obedient to the nocturnal beast he'd become. Behind his long, dark coat I could see the neckline of the cardinal-coloured top for which he'd become famous. His top wasn't famous then, you understand, and I only noticed it because I thought it was strange he was wearing a coat indoors in July, and that he wasn't in any of his usual collared shirts or one of the suits he wore to work. I often noted how M— dressed. He was stylish in a reserved way; and, one day, I used to tell myself, one day when I had the money, when I won it big on scratchcards or simply had a job, one day, I would dress like him. Red was a new colour for M—. I'd never seen him wear it before. It worked. It blazed darkly against his skin which, in the early evening light, looked smooth and warm, like dew-darkened terracotta catching the sun.

'I wanted to see if you were okay,' I told him in his doorway, 'and to say I didn't believe any of it and I'm sorry about Mum and I'm sorry it even happened. Any of it. All of it. And I hope I haven't upset you with this.'

Despite all of the time I'd spent rehearsing how I'd hand M— the paper in the same courteous fashion I imagined he would have handed it to me, I thrust it at him, face up. It flopped limply from the centre with a creasing sound that still makes my hair stand on end today.

M—, in his quiet way, asked me what it was. He read my letter then and there, in the front hallway. I like to think I looked at least a little proud.

When he finished reading he asked if I would like a cup of tea. 'I'm afraid,' he said, glancing toward the kitchen, 'we're out of biscuits.'

'We're not!' and before he could tell me not to bother, I dashed next door. Mum looked suspiciously at me when I told her what I was doing. Then it was as though she couldn't look at me at all. She was draining some pasta and the way the steam rose from the sink when Mum held the colander high and shook it made me think of how she said she'd seen M— at the supermarket a month or more back. She was surprised to see him with a whole trolleyful of food. 'Enough to bloody feed the bloody lot of them,' she'd said. It upset me, the thought of M— having to do his shopping all alone. Or really, I didn't care so much about the shopping. That was nothing. It was the idea of M— eating by himself that killed me. I grabbed all of our biscuits and headed out: I thought we could make a meal of it.

As I ran out of the kitchen, Mum shouted something after me that I didn't quite catch. It might have been something about 'snacking.' But knowing Mum, it may have been something insulting about M—.

I won't say it, but I'm sure you can guess the word.

Besides, whatever she did say, I didn't stop to hear. Not properly.

When I pushed open M—'s new front door (the old one had been shattered in the dawn raid) I was surprised to see he was exactly where I'd left him, leaning against the wall and reading the paper, only now his back was to me. M— must have been surprised too, because as I run in, he grabbed my neck. Doesn't even look. His arm whips round, lightning quick. Spins me face first into the wall: SMACK! Grabs my leg. My feet shoot up behind me. Up here, to where my chest should be. I'm sure I would have hit the floor hard, too, if M— doesn't suddenly yank my hood. He yanks so hard that it tears a little – just at the ends – where the drawstring would be if it hadn't disappeared in the wash.

I drop the biscuits.

Everything stops. There is a moment when I'm dangling there, suspended in mid-air. And then, as gently as you'd lower yourself into a hot bath, M— sets me back on my feet.

I start to run but M— sidesteps me and blocks the door. With a groan and his fists balled up, he rubs his eyes. 'Sorry. I'm sorry. I'm sorry …'

He looks like he is about to cry. So I touch his arm. M— stands aside, clearing a path for me. He draws his knuckles across his eyelids so that his skin is pulled outward, toward his ears, and I can see the whites and brown and the crimson of his eyes. The evening sun comes out from behind the clouds, shining in from the kitchen, down the hall, lighting M— from behind and the thousands of tiny dust particles that flit in the air around him. I don't know what mesmerises me more.

'Can you see the …?' He rubs his eyes again and blinks. I steal a peek at his eyes. M— is looking at me, into mine. So I look away.

'Do you see?' he asks. But I don't know what I'm supposed to be looking for. He isn't crying, there aren't any tears, so I take a step back and look down to see if he's dropped a contact lens. I hardly think I had it in my head that anything at all had happened, other than maybe M— lost a lens. I certainly wasn't thinking how M—, however mindlessly (but with certain certainty) had attacked me, or that I was in danger. I blocked it out. All I could think was how miserable he looked, how cut up he must be. His week in Paddington Green, the strip search, the bright lights, the questions, the questions, the questions, his parents, Tara, all the attacks in the news constantly reminding him of the night he opened his front door and ... I thought he'd snapped.

Amazing he could still speak.

And stand.

And breathe.

'Look,' he said quietly, pulling back his lids so I could see the orbits of his eyes. He lowered his head on level with mine.

That's when he told me. He said he got flashes in his eyes. He said he didn't understand it, didn't know why they came. They just did.

'They come,' he said taking a long while before saying anything more, as though he was trying to remember something recently forgotten. 'They come when I hear things off to the side ... or from behind. When I turn a corner or ... open a door.'

When the eyeflash lit up, he said, it was all he could see. Great bursts of light.

But there was nothing there. 'I don't see anything,' I said.

M— asked me to look again. He told me to look close. He dropped his hands, blinked, and rolled his eyes up into his head. He turned away and quickly spun round at me.

I'm ashamed to say there was a moment when I half thought he'd attack me again.

But he didn't; and the moment passed. I stood close, looking into his eyes. All I could see was the two of us standing there, looking at each other, in his front hall, near the stairs leading up to his bedroom, adjacent to mine. I thought we must look as though we were sharing some deep understanding, like we were in a film when the soundtrack starts up. Mahler or Gershwin or someone. Blondie. I thought how much I'd like a photograph of us. Just the two of us stood close, looking at each other, without any words, pronouncing the longest phrase.

But I didn't tell him that. I couldn't. So I didn't say anything at all.

M— stooped and collected the newspaper. He'd dropped it when I'd come bumbling back with the biscuits. I can't swear he'd been reading the article, but the front page headline was about a pensioner found dead in his flat, three streets away. A World War II veteran beaten to death while he slept. Iron pipes.

That's when it hit me. How could I have been so stupid? I'd burst through M—'s front door, finding him there, exactly where he'd been knocked unconscious and left for dead. Who wouldn't think I was *them*?

Wouldn't you?

Beginning on 12 July, it was as though M was making up for lost time. That very night he stepped from the shadows and saved Melanie Brinkman. Melanie, a sixteen-year-old schoolgirl, was returning home alone after a night out in the West End. She was blind drunk. Someone grabs her from behind. One hand over her mouth and the other between her legs. Dragged into the bushes, pushed to the ground in the darkened close beside the station. Face in the soil, skirt yanked up. She feels his weight behind her … and then everything lifts away. He's on top of her and then he's gone. Melanie is too sacred to look around. Too scared to scream. She hears a struggle, a man yell, 'No!' Footfalls. CCTV at the station was on the blink, but the man's body was found in the allotments backing onto the tracks. No ID, but a broken neck.

At 2:15a.m., not even two hours later, in Bernard's Lane, a residential street with a small wood on one side and a bus lay-by at its top end, Neil Watton was attacked by a gang of hooded youths. They circle round, punching the back of his head, his face; pull their knives, and demand his bus fares. Having finished his route five or ten minutes early, Neil had been urinating in the wood. Forced to hold his hands above his head he is marched, still urinating, back to the bus, when the knife suddenly disappears from his throat. Neil hurriedly zips up. He sees a passing figure in the wing mirror. When he looks around the figure is gone. Neil reported the man wore dark clothes, but for a flash of red.

At around 5a.m., Charles Kikwete, still in a cast, rose stiffly to make a cup of tea and switch on the wireless. The Shipping Forecast always soothed him back to sleep. But, seeing a shadow pass his kitchen window, he quickly dials 999. When the police arrive minutes later, they find a parcel outside Charles' garden door. Wrapped in the front section of the *Guardian* is his missing fake hand. It looks as though it had been exposed to the elements since it was stolen. Police examine it for fingerprints, but find none.

On 13 July, at around 3a.m., Bill Derwent was carried from the darkened railway arch where he'd been knocked off his motorbike. A hit and run. The man stays with Bill until the ambulance hoves into view. Paramedics report seeing a figure disappearing into the shadows. Later, in hospital, a night nurse reports that it's as though Bill, still unconscious, wants to say something, but can't finish his word. It sounds like he is humming. 'M-m-m-m,' is the only sound he makes.

On 14 July, near the library, Obifami Roberts, 14, was attacked by a gang. It's 10p.m.; Obifami is returning home from his girlfriend's. The gang beat him with fists and bricks. They kick him into a ball, knife his sides, and leave him for dead. CCTV picks up the gang scattering through the Sir Frederick Meyer estate. Twelve or so. Sprinting.

Three days later and, at the same casualty ward as Obifami, one of the gang members was admitted under 24-hour police guard. His lips have been sliced off. Press and police called him Boy X. Through his solicitor, he confessed to being present at, but only witnessing, Obifami's attack. Police traced footage of it to his mobile, a 90 second video. Obifami fly-kicked from behind. Obifami collapsing. Obifami surrounded: a rush of arms and fists and hoods. Laughing. But there was nothing detailing what happened two days later. Nothing but Boy X's lipless account of being grabbed from behind in his building's darkened stairwell.

He doesn't see who hammers his head on the metal dumpster. Doesn't see who tears off his hood before he can yell for help. The man holds him face first against the breeze block wall, and speaks quietly. He wants to know about the attack on Obifami. Who did it? He wants names. The man takes Boy X's mobile. Boy X tells him everything he knows. Word gets round that he squealed … and, the following night, two boys hold him down to his bed. The third has a pair if scissors. Boy X doesn't see their faces: their hoods are drawn tight. He doesn't see the fourth person, videoing everything, doesn't see the footage when it appears online within hours. A warning to others to keep their mouths shut. Police never recover his lips. Nor his mobile. But eight people are arrested for the attack on Obifami. Six turn themselves in and – get this – *all* reported their hoods forcibly removed within 48 hours of the attack. All! Every one of them!

M hit the papers. WHAM! He's everywhere. *Like that.*

M: four of the kids arrested for Obifami's attack reported seeing the letter. And there were half a dozen separate sightings on top of that. All in roughly the same area, a handful of postcodes. Press speculate M is only one letter of a longer word. A logo. A message, a statement about why he is doing everything he does. A telling or ironic self-appointed street name. AMORAL, MIMIC, TIMID, REMOVE, SAMARITAN, WIMP. All guesses. Conjecture. Bloggers speculate he wears a series of tops, with a different letter on each. They speculate there are letters on other articles of his clothing. His shoes, a hood or hat. His collars and cuffs and belt buckle. Stitched onto the back pockets of his jeans.

But nobody can remember what he's wearing. Just dark clothes. A red top. The letter M.

So, the police step it up: foot patrols, community support officers, police on bikes, on horses, outside the schools and on the high street. Plainclothes, undercover. Every third or fourth person is probably a cop. Like the Stasi or something. Reports flood in of young people whose hoods have been removed. By blade or simply ripped away. M is everywhere, on everyone's lips. SoLo Knight is swiftly dropped by everybody but the local paper.

They stick by it – at first. The editor says we mustn't forget the competition to name our local hero was a 'fair and democratic process', and that they haven't received any word from the SoLo Knight stating that he wants to be called anything other than what they've dubbed him.

I think what he meant to say is he didn't want to hurt the feelings of the competition winner, Little Davey Langdon.

But I didn't mind.

And I can't imagine he did either:

On 16 July, around 9p.m., David (now 12) was alone in the park when he is attacked. He is dribbling a football; his attackers wear hoods. They come at him from behind. Chase him. Beat him with fists and a pole, steal his iPod and mobile, push his face into the mud. They kick his football into the trees, warning him they'll kill his family if David doesn't count to 500 before getting up.

David counts to 89, when, out of nowhere, his football comes rolling up to his face. Later that night, he can't believe his ears when he hears his mobile signal an incoming text. It's been slipped through the letter box in the front door, along with his iPod. The text message originates from his own phone, and it reads simply: M.

ten

Two or three times a month, uniformed teams of two checked up on me. They wanted to see if I've tampered with the tag or monitor. They looked after the devices as though they were ailing relatives who they visited more out of obligation than love. Like the devices were people. The tag might as well have been a part of me, a special limb, but I treated the monitor as though it was a person too.

It was in the sitting room, on the bookcase where Mum kept her DVDs: a simple black box about the size and weight of my dictionary, with a digital clock on its face, telephone and buttons on top, and a range that spanned throughout the house. It knew when I was in bed, in the bath, the kitchen, in my room studying or snooping about online, or slung out in front of the telly. It knew when I wasn't there too – but I always kept my curfew. Always. Always-always-always. A promise as much to Mum as to myself. I didn't promise the monitor, although I did sometimes talk to it. 'Just getting something to eat – back in a flash.' 'How long have I been asleep?' 'Off for a whazz.' 'What do you say we stay in and watch a film tonight?' I double-checked its cords weren't loose, that its plug was plugged in. I checked its time against the pips on the radio and re-checked it against my mobile. Sometimes, when it was hot, the monitor would start to smell. I think it was the plastic casing. It smelled like a sweaty arse. So, on sunny days, I sprayed it with air freshener from the loo. Orange blossom.

The people who checked up on me were sometimes the same faces who'd visited before. But there was no telling who'd show up or when. Dawn, the middle of the night. Anytime. Their uniforms were vaguely official, like something you'd see on a supermarket security guard; and the checker-uppers were gruff, businesslike. Never staying long and never keen on talk. Visits lasted five minutes tops. Then I was alone again. Just me, my monitor and tag.

Except I knew I was never alone. I knew I was being watched.

M— was being watched, too. Although nobody knew he was the M all over the news, and so he wasn't being watched *per se*. M was being watched for, which is something altogether different.

It wasn't just the papers and the bloggers on the lookout. The police were gunning for him too. They demanded he come forward. They wanted to speak to him as a potential witness; question him about the forced removal of all those hoods. Thirty maybe even forty kids by now. Seemingly everyday. Every night, more and more. The police didn't say as much, but a few of the papers implied M's 'de-hooding' was a crime. Some bloggers said it outright. They called it bullying. A Met spokesman said:

> The police would like to speak with any persons knowing who might be responsible for these actions. While I cannot comment in detail on any particular case, I will say that the Met is prepared to offer full protection to any individuals who can bring about a dialogue with the person or persons responsible for these actions.

Asked if the police considered the de-hooded youths victims of crime, the spokesman declined comment. Which of course meant: yes. Definitely, yes. Definitely. But, you ask me, it also meant they thought they got what they deserved. The tables hadn't so much turned but were upended, legs snapped off and wielded like clubs. M won our hearts for that. People loved him for it. And he was crucified for it too.

On 18 July, police appealed for anyone witnessing the attack on Malcolm Richards. He was kicked to pieces on a night bus, the N188. The attack was unprovoked and happened two months earlier, in May, beginning at 3:17a.m. CCTV footage shows the assailant standing on a seat for leverage. He kicks Malcolm in the back of the head, his mouth, in the eyes. Stamps on his neck, stabs him in the groin. The assailant was in his mid-to-late teens, between 5'5" and 5'8". Malcolm's face bore the print of the attacker's shoe. Police issued an e-fit of the suspect. It was Ommie. Or rather it proved to be Ommie: the e-fit didn't look like him. Not much.

He looked like a kid.

He looked human.

Still, there must have been something in it that meant something to M—. The eyes, the cheekbones, his petulant Cupid's bow mouth. I don't know but for the e-fit whether M— could have found Lester, Ommie or Carl at all.

You need to know more about them. Who they were and what they did. I think I've already told you they called themselves LOCK Crazy Crew and that their berserk, wanton violence was feared even among the secondary members of their gang. Some people have a penchant for thuggery, for murder, for torture and rape. They plan it. They map it out, treat it like a craft. It *means* something to them. Others don't give a damn. To them it's simply a commodity, of sorts. Something to be used or spent, something disposable. Like a packet of crisps or a mobile phone or, I don't know, *a quid*. And they're the sort you have to watch out for. They're the ones to fear. Because they'll do anything, because they just don't care.

Lester, Ommie and Carl were like that. Or not 'like' that – they were *just* that. And because of it, celebrities. Forming letters with their fingers, schoolchildren pretended to be them, flicking through the four letters L-O-C-K and then making the sign of a gun. Forming inverted commas, government officials called them 'street'. Ex-street-gang members-turned–community-activists, while condemning LOCK Crazy Crew, said, when interviewed, that the gang was respected because 'they keep it real'. By that I think they meant they didn't put on airs. Lester, Ommie and Carl lived in a warren of disused council blocks and abandoned terraces, moving from one to another as they saw fit. They took over whole streets and estates. They didn't have to fight their way in. They just took. Families succumbed, were hobbled or simply kept indoors, kept their mouths shut. Say anything and your children were dead, scarred, raped, mutilated. Look at them the wrong way – look at them full stop – and you'd get the same. Buildings, shop fronts, churches, mosques, underpasses, street signs, and trees were tagged with their logo – a skull with a rounded bolt forming its jaw. It looked like a padlock, which I think must have been the point.

'LOC' stood for their names. And the 'K' was for 'Killers'. Because that's what they were. It's what they did. Because they didn't give a damn. They were beasts. They were ghoulish. They were ghouls.

What did they look like? The photos are few and many aren't clear. Lester and Carl were powerfully built, over six feet tall. Over tightly-drawn hoods, each wore a heavy padlock that swung from the thick, noosed chains around their necks. They made videos and posted them online (more about these later), jerking and thrusting and hand-signalling in a way that was as menacing as they were muscled. Ommie was smaller. My size. He was wiry and, I later read online, liked to carry a knife that was as long as his forearm.

I think it must have been him who killed M—'s mum. Whatever he used cut her clean through. Imagine the sound of it. Would it even make a sound? Something like when you make a hash of cutting a melon and have to tear it in two.

It's anyone's guess what M— thought. Could it really matter who did what to whom? Or perhaps he had something special in store for each of them? Perhaps, I like to think, he even *asked* them who did what to his mum, his father, to Tara – and then calmly told Lester, Ommie and Carl to choose what their punishment would be. That *was* their punishment. Not just what he did to them, but making them choose what he *would* do to them. What they would receive. Enforcing on them the wretched responsibility of self-mortal decision. He'd give them options; and all of them would be horrible.

I can see how he might have done that. Explained to them their choices, told them to pick the manner of their death, and then waited calmly, without moving, with unmannered certainty, for each to decide. For each to step forward and accept the brutal fate of his own choosing.

I can see that. But what I can't see is M— getting any pleasure from it. As much as I like to think he felt at least a little happiness in the time he spent with me, I have to wonder if he allowed himself to feel any pleasure at all.

Or if he could.

But perhaps he slipped up once or twice? After all, I did see him smile, I saw him laugh.

And perhaps he felt at least a *little* pleasure when LOCK Crazy Crew started to slip up. Or if not exactly slip up, when M— could finally begin forming a picture of who killed everyone he loved.

There was the e-fit of Ommie.

There were whatever scraps of information M— had forced from Boy X before the gang sliced off his lips.

And, a few weeks later, nearer when everything came to an end (and I would never see M— again), there must have been clues, somewhere, in the boasting, menacing and often near unintelligible LOCK Crazy Crew videos on YouTube, LiveLeak, YourClipz, and about half a dozen other websites. Places you go only if you know where to look. Or if, like me, you're trapped indoors night after night and find yourself trawling through blogs and chat rooms, these obscure underground news sites and portals that direct you somewhere else, to some site rigged up in some council block bedroom only last week to feature ultraviolence downloaded from mobiles. Rants and threats and conspiracy theories cobbled together and posted by people who, by the simple token of owning or having access to a computer, understand this as nothing less than immitigable evidence of having something important to say. *Anything* to say.

Stephen, I ask you, what happened to talent? What happened to *recognising* talent? To developing it? What happened to *celebrity*? I don't care if it makes me sound elitist – and I know how much you like your IT geekery, the worldliness of the Interweb – but, you ask me and 99% of those sites should be shut down for their bald artlessness and pot noodle insightfulness.

You won't catch me doing any of that blogging business. Tweeting and things. Oh, no. I have a story to tell. This is the real thing. I was *there*.

The LOCK Crazy Crew videos: rank, fearless, fearsome and horrifying. And arrogant. An arrogance that, in the end, proved tantamount to a confession. Revelatory. A trail not leading right to their door but near enough for M—, with his watchfulness, his near invisibility and serpentine silence, to figure out which was theirs. And one night, perhaps when they were at their most narcissistically and murderously inflated, wait for them behind it.

Did they do it on purpose? Did they make the videos to taunt, if not specifically M, but also their victims and the families of their victims and all of their victims-to-be? To antagonise as much as to be recognised, no matter – not to make this sound like any of the raps they barked in their videos – no matter how heavily disguised? It's funny how people give themselves away. Subconscious and all that. LOCK Crazy Crew? I don't know. Perhaps they couldn't help it. Perhaps they could see M was circling closer and closer – their vanity wouldn't have let them believe he was hunting anyone but them – and so wanted to demonstrate their savageness, their eminence and invincibility. Chest thumping before the showdown at high midnight.

Or, much as it pains me to say, perhaps Mum was on to something when she said people sometimes do things just to get caught. She said it not long after we'd moved next door to M—. When there were still boxes to unpack. Painting and dusting and polishing and things. Put the pictures up. Dad was gone and Mum was more or less back from the brink. She'd gone mental. She wouldn't wash – and now: 'People do things only to get caught'? It sounded mental. It *sounded* like a load of bollocks. I was too stunned to even shake my head, let alone tell her how mental it sounded. I mean, a person who steals something, steals it for a reason: because they want it, or … or maybe because they're bored. Because there and then, when they steal that something, there's nothing better to do than steal it. People steal things for kicks or just simply because they want something. *Not* because they want to get caught.

But the way Mum couldn't look at me when she said it – or rather, the way she didn't look at me, the way she looked as though she thought she'd not said anything but had simply thought something to herself – well, it got me thinking. Mum said what she said and went to bed. It was late, after twelve, so I knew she'd be out cold; she'd been doing up the house all day and getting nowhere with any of it. I poured myself a glass of her wine (and then another), helped myself to some of the raisin cake I'd seen her stash in the cupboard above the fridge-freezer, and thought: maybe sometimes people steal things not because they want it or want a bit of fun, but because they can use it to get something better. Trade up. They know stealing is wrong. They know it's better not to steal. They know it's wrong but something in their head is saying 'Go ahead, kiddo, steal it anyway.' Something is telling them to do something wrong so that – and only so that – they get the thrill of *maybe* getting caught. But then they *get* caught. And then, when it's all done, they can do something good again. They knew it all along: it's what they were after. They don't want to steal. They don't want to do something wrong. They want something good, something better. It's *why* they steal. I don't know if that makes sense, but … Stephen, do you see? You want to trade up something bad for something good.

What that does or doesn't say about people being inherently evil – or balanced intrinsically by an innate and shared notion of what's good – I can't say. All I can really say is Mum said something like that to me. People want to get caught.

I wish she'd said it sooner than she did.

I say I'd been in trouble before I was tagged. It's true. This is the dirt. It was just after Dad left and when Mum was busy going mental. I stole things and didn't give them back. I never hurt anyone. I never kicked in anyone's head or sloped about stabbing people in the ear. I just stole things and never gave them back.

What? All sorts. I stole a lawnmower once; tipped it into a pond. I stole bicycles and wallets and about a hundred things from shops: crisps, sweets, condoms, biscuits, Lucozade, I dunno – *milk*. Things I didn't want or have any use for. Dresses left to dry on washing lines, mobiles, street signs, bags, toys, a dummy from a baby, a buggy (it was empty), books, fresh fruit, cured meats, my teacher's keys, handbags, the socks and kecks of the other boys when we were at swim class ...

And I got caught, too. Many times. Often. A lot. So often that I got excluded from school. I got excluded from school so often that Mum told me she talked to her therapist about it. Or really, I got excluded from school so often that Mum broke down and told me she'd broken down to her therapist about me. Her therapist said I wanted to get caught. And maybe I did. Yes, I'll admit that: maybe I did. But I didn't like hearing it. I didn't like hearing what Mum's therapist had to say about me. I only wished Mum would get better, that she'd be sane, and Dad would come home. Or at least talk to me. His silence was terrible. It was really-really ... bad. I didn't like it. And I didn't like it any better that Mum wanted to send me to a therapist. Like I was crazy. She said we couldn't afford two therapists. Mum said she would have to stop seeing hers if I didn't stop stealing.

So I did. I stopped stealing things and not giving them back. I didn't steal again. Not even kisses. I kept that *right* out of the picture, completely away from anything I thought or did or ...

... Yes, so, in that way, I don't think I really stopped stealing from me.

It kills me to say, but M— did things too. I've never told anyone this, but M— did things he probably shouldn't have done. Okay, maybe not as bad as ... Look, whatever he did I don't think he did any of it to get caught. Not him. He did it to trade up for a greater good – even if the greater good was selfish, if it was ultimately for him, for his parents and Tara. The hoods were only the start. He stripped them free with his hands or with whatever was *at* hand: their knives, the utility razors they used on each other. I know it was M—. *I know.* And I know it was him who marked all those kids, too. Have I told you this? Big letter Ms across their faces. First it was the hoods – the hoods, you have to figure, because he wanted to see their faces, to see if they were *them.* And then the lettering. UV dye, indelible ink, ballpoint, that juice you get in glow sticks. He cut off their hoods to see who they were; marked them – a branding, really – so he'd know them again. Perhaps he thought he'd recognise who'd cracked him with the bat. Perhaps he saw the other two looming down the hall. I think he must have seen something, otherwise I don't know how he could have even got started.

He never told me.

But the de-hooding, the big letter Ms. I think he must have thought that when his eyeflash went bursting off, it was telling him he'd got it right. That he found them. Or maybe … maybe he got all of that wrong.

I think he may have done. I think he did. Or maybe it's *me* who's wrong. I don't know. I really don't know if I've got it right. I don't know if I've figured it out, not all of it.

But, the fact is, nobody else comes close. It's one of the big mysteries how everyone who saw M – people who he trapped, de-hooded, branded or saved – never remembered his face. But I know how he did it. I've got the answer. After LOCK Crazy Crew murdered Tara and his parents, M— was borne by a warped probity. It was something shrouded, buried, fiendish, something ordinarily suppressed and, because it was all of these things, inherent. As much a part of him as it is a part of anyone. It guided him from within, which is something (I suppose we can call it) superheroic, if only in the sense that he managed to overcome the inclination to silence it and instead allowed it to broker his ability to concede to it. Give in to it and it takes you over. Like some sort of second skin, an outer layer that both armours and disguises. Who could see past it? *Who?* Who could describe with accuracy someone cloaked so convincingly by something so innate? The criminals wore hoods, bandanas, balaclavas, baseball caps pulled low. M— wore something immeasurably more disguising. He wore his inner-self: the monster he became.

If there was anything that gave the game away, if there was anything that told the world who he was, it was the letter M. Wearing it, marking people with it. He wasn't the sort you'd think had it in him. But then vanity – or the altogether human wants of recognition and individuality – is something we can't shrug off, not completely. It always surfaces. It's inside; worms its way up through you, to the top. Marks you. Your skin and eyes. There for the world to see. Like a brand.

On 20 July, Petr Kalinowska, 28, was stabbed in Farrow Road. He died at hospital. Police arrested a 13-year-old boy three streets away when they saw him attempting to hide the red letter M covering his face. There is blood on the back of his top where his hood had hung. His neck is cut. The wound is superficial, but the boy's mum kicks off, demanding publicly that the police arrest whoever slashed her son.

Boy X's mum was more outspoken. She gets her own Max Clifford and demands an independent inquiry into the police department's 'inability' to arrest the people who had mutilated her child. Gets a special section in the local paper for a petition that whips up something like seven, eight hundred signatures, and that bears her son's photograph, taken at a christening, before the attack. In a televised and tearful rant, she says M is responsible for disfiguring her son.

But 700 people! 700 people supported this! *And* they gave her money. Something like two thousand pounds. For … *For*? You've got to remember that nobody challenged her outright. Nobody. When everybody should have dismissed it out of hand, they handed over their money. For medical bills? For new lips? For her, I tell you. For the mum. So she could see herself on telly in a new hat and frock. Recognition. Fame. Fame and pity – or fame as a consequence of pity. Why? She was a victim too, she said. She trilled and wept all over the news, this shopfront solicitor-cum-media-advisor by her side. She was indignant. She had a point (I'll concede): things couldn't have been easy for her. Things must have been pretty fucking tough. But a *victim*?

She wasn't up to scratch. Not a sausage. Not against the real thing.

On 22 July, at around 2a.m., three people entered 77 Saintbury Close, where the Singhs, 29 and 34, were asleep. The intruders reach through the cat flap and find the key hanging nearby. They kill the cat, swiftly, with a bat. Ranjit hears it and investigates. They beat him to death. His wife, Maharani, is tied to the bedrail, stripped, beaten and knifed. Raped by all three, using themselves, the baseball bat that killed Ranjit, and Ommie's giant knife. Maharani tops herself two months later. Police couldn't find a motive for the attack, save for robbery. The cameras Ranjit used as a documentary filmmaker were stolen.

On 25 July, three people in hoods attacked Jalandhar Ghosh behind the Abrakebabra, where he worked with his uncle and cousin. It's something like two in the morning, the pubs are shut, and Jalandhar goes out back with the last of the evening's recycling when he's shot in the throat. They shoot his uncle and cousin too. Only the uncle survives. The assailants wear black bandanas covering their faces, steal £400, call him a Paki bastard and all that. Blame him for bombs.

On 26 July, Sam Kulawanea, a 16-year-old asylum seeker from Sierra Leone, was cornered by a hooded youth outside Costcutters. The kid threatens Sam with a screwdriver, demanding he give him his money and mobile. Sam's got fuck-all; he lives in a hostel. CCTV footage, beginning at 23:11, shows the youth trying to stab Sam, when a figure appears in the bottom corner of the screen. Police suspect the person must have said something, because the attack on Sam stops.

It shifts.

Two days later it was front page news. National press, Scottish editions, regional papers, local advertisers … everywhere. Goes like this. Sam runs some short distance off when his attacker lunges for the mysterious figure. But, hearing a yell, he glances back. He doesn't catch the man's face, but describes him as over six feet tall and wearing a dark coat. He sees a flash of red. CCTV footage doesn't add anything. Just shows the back of someone's head. The figure has dark-dark hair and doesn't advance. The hooded youth goes for him. It's grainy and lasts only a few seconds. And it's as alluring as it is alarming when both the man and the hooded kid disappear from sight. Edge of your seat until 23:13, when the attacker sprints diagonally across the screen. His hood is missing and he's cradling his hand. We don't see the man again. In the printed press, his head is circled in red. On TV, it's haloed. And no matter where it's featured it's accompanied by a statement from the Chief Superintendent:

> While I cannot comment directly on these events, it is a matter of public concern when an individual takes the law into his or her own hands. The Met is doing everything in its power to tackle crime and to make our communities safer. It is in the best interest of the general public that we should do our job without interference from individuals lacking proper law enforcement training.

I watched the footage again and again. I clipped probably four dozen photos from the papers. Free papers, local papers, quality nationals, tabloids. Front page, frame by frame stills, blow ups and small. I couldn't tell for certain, but there was something familiar about the man's head. Or at least it seemed familiar because the first person I thought of was M—.

You ask: did I want it to be him?

The answer – and the real question – is how could I know for sure?

That's why and when I decided to get a picture of M—. No matter what, I'm getting my photo: his photo. It was the only way I'd ever know for certain.

Just thinking about it was enough to make me sick.

eleven

What bothered me so much about taking the photo? Was it that there was some great secret in danger of being made public? (Like me, I wouldn't allow myself to think, being outed.) Was it because I was worried I'd be lumped together with and marked down as another of these out of control hoods, someone to be feared, even though I'd done nothing to get in trouble since I was tagged? Was it because if it was M— who'd saved Sam, it would define the difference between him and me, between the good and the criminal, a line swiped down the middle with us on either side?

Or was it that I felt betrayed by M—? He saved me, he saved my life *twice*, but now he's doing it for others too?

I needed him. I needed to know he could still save me. You see …

Right, it had been several weeks since the man in the woods, but the attack went on and on in my head. Foolish of me maybe, but I told myself it would go away. I thought – or maybe it's better to say I hoped – it would disappear. But it didn't: it grew. In my head, the man came after me again and again. Forcing me to strip. Beating me. Beating off. And me – what do I do? What did I do? Nothing. Not a thing. Why? *Why?*

For I-don't-know-how-long, I tried for a false memory. Tried remembering things so that I actually put up a fight, really whacking him one. I get this sudden strength out of nowhere and smash him in the teeth. He drops and I kick him like those kids kicked David Langdon's football. But I don't kill him. He lives. That's the crazy thing: in my false memories, I always spare his life. *And make sure he knows it.*

So there we have it. I tried for the false memory, tried my damnedest. I told myself I was okay, that I'd survived. But I didn't buy it. Not a bit. I looked for the man everywhere. Or maybe because I wasn't actually *looking* for him, I saw him everywhere. I scrutinised men's faces. I ran a mile every time I heard the rattle of a dog chain. Thought every man climbing upstairs on the bus was him. Every man queuing at the newsagent's, every man sitting in a car, lingering outside the bookies, in the crowds behind news reporters on telly, or talking low on a mobile as he breezed past our house. I thought he'd tracked me down. And now M— was where? Too busy! Too busy saving someone else. Not me: *someone else*. Whenever I thought I saw the man, I wanted to scream. It was right here, in my throat, hot as broth. I'd go dizzy. I passed out so many times, I hate to think. And so, after a while, all I did was stay in. I didn't leave home unless I absolutely had to. I didn't say as much to myself (or to M— or Mum or even to Darrell Thomas), but what I was really doing was trying to hide. Or not even that. I wasn't trying. I was hiding, full stop.

Look, you've got to understand I was kind of okay at the start. I mean that: it's true. Those first few days and I ignore it. Put it right out of my head and instead focused on my studies and everything in the news. M— said he'd sorted it and M— isn't the sort who makes things up. M— doesn't lie. Not him. He says I shouldn't worry; I believe him. Or at least, convince myself I do. And three, maybe four days later I line up all of Mum's toiletries and lather and exfoliate and shampoo and scrub and scrub until the hot water runs out. I'm ready to face up to things, stare them down. I head for the hilltop park. It's overcast, windy and there's a fine, spitting rain. I try and find some beauty in it. Standing just inside the park gates, I look for birds. I run my eyes along the grassy swell of the hill, the tumble of clouds, the greens, yellows and reds and the many shapes and blossoms of the bushes and ornamental trees ...

But when a car door slams somewhere behind me, I leg it. Go, pelting through traffic, straight home. Shoving past buggies and fat waddlers. In the street, on the pavement, over guardrails.

Blind. Mad with fear. So scared, I've got to double-check the locks are locked twice once I lock myself in. I put the chains on. I test the locks on the windows. Check for faces in the windows. With a kitchen knife in one hand, and Mum's little nail scissors in the other, I throw open my wardrobe, Mum's wardrobe, the little utility cupboard under the stairs, stabbing in the dark. I check under the beds, behind the couch, behind the doors where there isn't room for a shadow to hide. Then I run through the whole circuit again. All the openings; I check the doors and windows more often than I like to admit. Everything is secure, but I still don't feel safe. Not even when I huddle up against the wall between M—'s and my bedrooms. The wall is cold. As though he isn't there.

Like he's abandoned me. Like Dad.

I hate him for it. *Hate him.* I buy a Fast Cash and a Goldrush and don't win a thing.

After that, very nearly all the going out I do is going next door and looking for M— or visiting Darrell Thomas, and that's only because I have to.

Now, Darrell. Maybe there's more to say about him than I first thought. Darrell could tell something was wrong. Or, to be one hundred per cent truthful, I thought I could tell that he could tell something was wrong. He would glance at me out of the corners of his eyes whenever he banged out an email, or knocked together answers for whatever form was up on his screen. Kept turning to me to say something, but not saying a word and turning away again. It was as though he thought I'd re-offended, or just gone and done something stupid. At one of our meetings, after the CCTV footage of M was splashed all over the place, Darrell, not for the first time I can assure you, started bearding me.

'It is true,' he said, with his hands steepled before him and his Arsenal tattoo leaping all over the shop, 'That man oft not understands his actions. But let it be said that all men know always their actions, for each is a purposeful act of individual consciousness.'

'Darrell –'

'Do you have something you want to tell me?'

The door to Darrell's office was closed. It was raining, so the room was heavy with cigarettes. He'd been leaning out the window when I came in; water droplets still glistened atop the matted knots of his hair. But above the smoke, above Darrell's aftershave, I could smell the hall outside his office door. Whenever it rained, the ceiling leaked, leaving long, fallow stains down the walls and damp patches on the carpet. The carpet was red, for what it's worth, artery red, and so thin it didn't look rolled out so much as spread. The hallway – running in either direction from his door and leading to about half a dozen more cramped offices with another Darrell and another me in each – smelled catty. Like some alley cat rocked up whenever it needed a wazz. Now that I think about it, perhaps that's why Darrell smoked. Or at least why he smoked so often. To cover the scent.

This is England. It always rains.

'Why don't you just say it?' Darrell paused, before almost whispering, 'I promise it'll be okay. Trust me.'

I couldn't look at him. If I did I'd give myself away. I couldn't look at him but I knew Darrell was staring at me. We'd been through this little routine again and again. It was easier not to look Darrell in the face from the start than it was to look at him and have to look away when he started in on me. Every few days – and almost always after taking a phone call or some of his two-fingered hammering at the PC – he would start by asking if I had something to tell him. Like he already knew something and expected me to fess up. He would clear his face, fold his hands and look deep into me. Knowingly. Really annoyingly. Sometimes, he'd raise his eyebrows. Sometimes, nod to himself or pretend he was forced to censor whatever it was he wanted to say. At first, I thought it was simply his way. An invitation to talk. Open up. But, after the first few times, I spotted the pattern: I had to think he was asking me to come clean about something. What exactly, I didn't know – or at least didn't want to think about. Only thing making that day different was there were things I could tell him. About M— and how much I wanted to know (and was reluctant to find out) if he was the M all over the news. When I wasn't re-imagining everything in the woods, or busy with coursework, or following everything in the papers, just about the only thing I thought about was M—.

I didn't see everything was connected. I didn't see they were all one and the same.

Call it stupidity. Call it, I don't know, *youth*. I don't care.

But yes: 'Why won't you tell me?' Darrell unlatched his fingers and started spinning a pen round and round like gamblers do with gambling chips in films. He always did that when he wanted a cigarette but had to wait.

I suppose I shrugged. 'Nothing to say.'

'But there is: The Truth.'

'You want me to tell you I've done something wrong?'

'Wrong?'

'Isn't that what you're asking?'

'Am I?'

Sam Kulawanea's attacker was arrested at his mum's. Sixteenth floor in the Hayward Estate. Or something like that. Way up. Hospital staff tipped off the police. The boy's wrist was like muesli. He was ten days shy of his fifteenth birthday, and stuck to his story that he had been assaulted by a gang of youths. *That's* how he broke his wrist. He said they attacked him for 'giving them the evils'. There were six of them, but he didn't see any of their faces. Didn't recognise them. They wore hoods. And did he say a word about the mysterious man on CCTV?

Did he *fuck*. Because he denied he had been there at all.

The magistrate didn't buy it. Nor anyone else. Everybody with even half an eye could see he was the boy who'd attacked Sam. Or, because he was wearing a hood when he did, could see he was the same boy when he re-appears on screen. His hood and the screwdriver are missing, and he has to cradle one hand in the other as he sprints away. The police hunted for his hood and weapon but couldn't find either.

Maniac, read one headline.

Tooled you, ran another.

It's a thug, it's a lame, it's …

And everyone asked: Was it M?

And with one voice everyone, press included, answered: Yes. Oh, yes.

Only thing was, some of the press said M had assaulted the boy. People read it and started saying it too. They said the boy was a victim. You've probably heard all about the Hayward Estate – before they tore it down, I mean. Overcrowded and violent. Junkies. Squats. Faeces-laden stairwells. Practically Third World. The boy lived there with, I don't know, half a dozen of his extended family. He'd been excluded from school. Couldn't read, could add; didn't have a job or any training. All that. And so do they blame his parents – or at any rate, do they blame his mum for letting him run about like a jackal?

No, his mum was portrayed with this aching, almost desperate sympathy. Crying on telly and clutching at relatives to so much as stand up and … the works. So she's off the hook, and they point the finger at society and, in a half-arsed way, at 'young people today'. They say Social Services should have intervened. They say Social Services scored an own goal. They blame popular music, TV, film and video game violence. They say while the boy – and I remember this – they say while the boy should be supported to own up to 'whatever his wrongdoings were', he had been 'failed by the system'.

Failed by the system? As if he wasn't a part of it, Stephen! As if he, by birthright, wasn't *part* of 'the system'. But no. They don't think so. They said he 'slipped through the cracks'. A handful of council officials and charities called for an independent investigation. They got it, at the cost of half a billion pounds or something. I mean, couldn't they use that money for, I don't know, something better? Like … like just about anything.

I should cocoa.

But what really got my back up were those who said that if M would attack a 'lost lad' of such 'socio-economic disadvantage' then there was every reason to believe he would come for the rest of us, because we actually had something to lose. It was only a matter of time.

Yes, maybe I hated M—. Maybe I was angry with him. But the important thing is that it was around then that I must have started thinking more and more that M was M—. I mean, why else would I get so upset? The way people turned on him: bloggers, the press. All those nasty gits chucking their 2p into any old Interweb site, calling for him to come forward, and screaming for his arrest.

It still gets to me today, right here, inside. It still kills me.

And the other thing, I guess, that's just as important is the CCTV footage. It was the turning point. *The* turning point. Proof positive M existed. Until then, he was no better than a phantom. A myth, like the Beast of Sydenham or Spring-heeled Jack. CCTV not only revealed something about how he looked, but also something *about* him. He was too smart to reveal himself fully, to be seen, top to toe, on screen. Most people would go a step too far, give themselves away. But he's too smart for that: he's calculating. You see him, but you can't see him.

But what you *do* see is the rot inside. Look hard, look deep and you could see that part of him that was already dead.

I knew it was him. But of course, I didn't. I just I thought I knew.

Or let me rephrase that: I wondered. I wondered about M—. What did he make of everything? What went on in his head? In his heart? He must have been splintered inside. Every time he switched on the telly or slunk past a newsstand, he must have been reminded of what had happened in his home. How could he not be? How could he miss it? There was violence everywhere. Attacks. Hoods sliced. Necks slashed. Every night, there was more and more. Every day, there was a night.

And me? I was like one of those obsessives you read about, with a thousand photographs wallpapering some bare-bulbed bedroom. My PC might have been ancient (it could take several minutes to download so much as a single photograph), but I had dozens of stills saved on my hard drive. Stills and video. And dozens more photos cut from the papers. I mounted them in a sketchbook. In another, I drew them again and again. Drawing helped me think. It helped me think things through. Puzzle them out. And kill time. Bit by bit, I started turning the head of the man caught on CCTV. Turning him, so you could begin to make out the curves of his nose, the hollows of his eyes. And then, too, from the view of the boy, from angles all over the shop: up and down and from the side.

The mysterious face.

The darkened, unreadable eyes.

The weighted lip caught in a sliver of streetlight.

The shadows that blurred and cloaked.

A flash of red. The letter M.

I drew him again and again. Everything. And eye by lip by hand by chin, I drew M—. Call it fantasy. Call it hiding indoors day and night, but he was the only person I could picture rescuing me. Who else then could I picture rescuing Sam Kulawanea? Or any of the others? But *M*—? M— is M? *M*—? It was mad. Ab-so-lutely barking.

If only I had his courage: how he must pick himself up off the floor everyday.

If only I had his style: how he managed to look so clean, so beautiful, despite …

If only I had the guts to take his photograph. That's what I really wanted. Drawing him was one thing, but a photograph was the real deal. As much for me, you point out, as to see if he was *him*. I imagine you know your Freud and your Jung and your … It feels a bit like that today, you in your armchair and me rabbiting away from the chaise longue like a … Christ, how much Wodehouse can one have? It's like a forest in here. People must send them to you.

The week after the attacks on Petr and Sam, twenty young people were de-hooded. Hoods sliced and ripped. Never seen again. Six or seven have their arms snapped. Two get their clavicles (there's another word I like: sounds like an old-fashioned car) shattered to bits. All of them were marked with big letter Ms across their faces. All of them. Couldn't get it off. Some go on telly with their faces pixelated; it was strange how they wore their wounds like badges. Like a special, inverted honour. Their ticket to celebrity.

You see the same with electronic tags. People turn up their jeans and, as they cycle or strut past, the tag is right there, above their little-bitty sports socks. Like a medal.

Cui bono, so the saying goes.

Or more to the point (in our Freudian Age): *Honey, I'm still free. Take a chance, take a chance on me.* Abba for you. They know the world and its parts.

Just so we're clear, you didn't see that with me. Oh no. I hid my tag. I wanted rid of it. I counted the days until I'd be free. An eternity, until there was around a month to go. Then it seemed all the more interminable. Or worse – like something was about to go wrong. Any time, anywhere; something would cock up and the fault would be mine. Always-always mine. I'd do something stupid. The police would arrest me. I'd go to jail. I had a real fear of that. It wasn't only what I knew would happen to me *in* jail, but also what would happen when I got out. Who'd want me then? Where would I live? Who'd talk to me? If I went to prison, was it because I wanted to get caught? Was Mum *right*?

I had to talk myself down. Three or four times a week I would boil into such a panic that I'd get the dry heaves. Or just cry. Cry and cry. Soft as it makes me sound, but beginning some time in July, what with all the butterflies about, I'd tell myself I was like one of them. In a cocoon but, before I knew it, I'd be in the clear. Fluttering over clovered vales, in the sunlight, away and away and …

Beautiful to think about, isn't it?

Beautiful, even if it is a cliché.

What M— must have thought, with his name all but spelled out in the news, I really don't know. *M for Madman*, ran the headline. *Man or Menace? Mangled! Mutilator!* Online was a plethora more. Monsterinthedark.blogspot.com. Mformayhemblog. co.uk. MforMaster.com. MasonWatch.org. And something like a dozen or more websites had the CCTV clip of him alongside mobile phone happy slaps and people getting kicked down in schoolyards, on buses, the high street, under railway arches. All over the shop.

In that way, you've got to understand people were starting to see M and me as the same. There was no difference, no line drawn in the tarmac, to urbanise the phrase, with us on either side. *We* were the threat. *We* were the danger. I'm ashamed to say it comforted me. It was as if M— wasn't as distant as I'd thought. It brought us closer.

Kicker is how great it felt. It just about killed me.

But, knowing M—, I have to imagine it was nothing like the ride he got in his own head. Imagine the urgency! Imagine getting it wrong again and again! Everything he did, he did for real. That is, everything counted all the time. LOCK Crazy Crew could have been anyone to him. Anyone and everyone he confronted, or who came at him at night. He's hunting them and his eyeflash suddenly sparks off. Blinds him. Possesses him. Bewilders him. Opens him up to the unshakeable fiend inside that he no longer has the strength, probably not even the will, to suppress. He knows they don't see him coming. Don't see him, don't hear a thing. Next thing he knows, they're face down, their bloodied hood in his hand, their neck sliced, and there's not a sound in his head save for the wet snap of their clavicle splitting like the Earth.

Imagine. Imagine, Stephen. The frustration. Getting it wrong every night. Night after night after night. Everything he got wrong, every night. Months of it. Months! The better part of valour might be discretion but, you ask me, sometimes one hundred per cent of heroism can be flat out madness.

It must have eaten away at him.

He wasn't the only one.

The police got a right proper grilling. Who murdered Tara and M—'s parents? Who shot Ashley Taylor as he lay coughing his lungs up in the bath? Who gang raped Kelly Johnson and set her body alight while her daughter plummeted from the bathroom window and her husband was arm deep in guts and gauze in Iraq or Afghanistan or wherever? They couldn't tell you. They couldn't say.

And they couldn't tell you anything about M. He was simply – and in their parlance – a 'person of interest'. Meaning they wanted him bad. No matter what they could or couldn't, did or didn't say, they were getting it in the neck. It was all over the telly. Their thin lips and fevered eyes. Squinting with sweat and migraines. Offering *what*? Empty assurances that even *they* didn't buy. They'd never seen anything like it. Completely, utterly lost. Could kiss their careers away; their pensions; the lot. And, because of this, desperate, absolutely desperate and pissed off. No question about it. Pissed. Off. This was the States, they'd gun him down. BANG. Dead in his tracks.

Instead:

On 25 July, Charles Heber, 35, was beaten to death for £5 and his mobile.

On 27 July, David Dickens, 17, was stabbed eight times with a giant knife.

On 28 July, Marcel Henry, 15, was shot in the face.

On 30 July, Teddy Ashton was robbed at gunpoint. Teddy, 32, had parked his car outside the Co-op cash point in Croxley Road. It's one in the morning. He gets his money and a hooded man sticks a gun in his ribs. Teddy gives him the cash but passes out when he's forced to hand over his car keys. When he comes to, he's surprised to see his car is where he left it. His keys are in his hand and so is his £80. His assailant is lying feet away, de-hooded and unconscious. Police found blood from his broken face on the wall beside the cash machine. And the gun under Teddy's car. An imitation weapon that looked like the real thing.

At the exact same time, and only six streets away, police and paramedics rushed to the home of Neville Stubbs. Neville, 47, lost three teeth fighting his attackers. They stabbed him in the buttocks, the face, his back and shoulders. The pelvis. Legs. Everywhere. Take his laptop, mobile, £120 in cash. His sitting room is as damaged as his mouth, the walls spray-painted with 'BATTY' and 'BUMBOI' and a giant skull with a bolt forming the jaw, the word LOCK where its teeth should be. All four and half minutes of Neville's attack go online before dawn. There were three of them. CS gas, a knife, a bat, six fists. Four and a half minutes of it. Four and a half minutes is a lifetime when you're being beaten to death. Count it out. I could barely sit through the whole video.

Neville didn't die, I should say.

No, he still lives at 58 Stillman Terrace.

M— lived at number 22.

Mum and I, of course, were right next door.

Ready? Here we go. M—: you can imagine how all of *that* must have smacked him cold. Only doors down the street. When I saw him the next day, his eyes looked bruised. Big dark rings in the hollows and the rest of his face drawn and dry as cheese. It was nearing my curfew. There was maybe an hour of light left. And when I saw M—, I wanted to laugh.

Now maybe that sounds funny, but two things. First, all that day and all the previous night, I'd been going wild trying to see if he was okay. I knocked on his door, tried the bell, and kept lookout when he didn't answer. Not quite twenty-four hours straight but … Night before and everything kicks off as I'm heading to bed. The police come screaming up and, if I'm honest, my first thought is that they've come for me. The monitor's conked out or something: they're going to arrest me. But I check and it's okay, plugged in and all that. So I go for it: The Horrors. The police are here for the man from the woods. He's found me. Hunted me down. He's outside the window, the garden door. *He's already in the house.* Mum's home, but now she's going to find out what happened. He's going to rape me. He'll rape Mum. He'll kill us both. He'll …

But no. No, no. M—'s sorted it, I keep telling myself like a superloon And M— doesn't lie. So, *of course* the cops are for next door. The killers have come back and M— is all alone.

Except they go roaring past: six, seven cars, a van, an ambulance. And there's a helicopter with a spotlight circling round and round and low enough that you can see it below the clouds. I'm outside by now, on the front step; and when I see the police jammed up further down the street, I'm over the moon. It's not the sort of thing you're supposed to admit, is it? Not just not admit, but not feel full stop. Do you know what I mean? You're overjoyed, you're buzzing, when you see that whatever's happened, happened to someone else.

I was, at any rate. M—'s safe and so am I. Mum too. And even if the man from the woods is out there, if he's near, he can't do a thing because the police have taped everything off maybe thirty metres down.

You can picture it. The terraced street with everyone piled in front of their houses. It's dark; police lights bouncing. Angry drivers are seven or eight deep and want to turn around, but the street is too tight with parked cars and so they have to reverse back up the slope. But, even with all the people and all the cars and lights and this ... this *deleterious* pulse in the air, everything is still. It's quiet. And there's me, dangling my tagged ankle inside the front door and trying to see what's happening but I can't quite see over M—'s hedge. His lights are on. All the lights at the front of his house. And his is the only house where no one's watching the street.

So, already ablaze with irrationality, I flip-flop and think the worst: what if he's dead? If M— really is M, what if he's caught up with everything down the road? What if there's been another break-in, another attack and M—, being M, was uncannily there? Look, what's crazier: M— showing up for someone else from out of nowhere like he did twice with me and, I'm seriously starting to think, with Sam Kulawanea and others too, or me thinking M— is M? What if he happened onto something by chance and got hurt? Or is dying or dead or ... What if he was *caught*? Don't forget, he's got the red letter M on his chest, and now there's a knife in his gut, and the paramedics point it out to the cops who nail him for everything. The hoods, the brandings, the broken clavicles, broken faces, Melanie Brinkman's dead rapist, and for snapping that kid's wrist just off screen. Match the CCTV footage of the back of his head against the real thing and ... Bob's your uncle.

That's the other reason why I want to laugh when I, in full-on sulk the day after everything down the street, see M— in his garden. It's not simply that I see he's alive and not in jail or hospital or anything. It's more because I've been trying to take his photo without him seeing me. But had I seen him? Not the once. I'd gone round again and again, but he was never there. Or at least he never came to the door. Perhaps I didn't wait long enough? After a few seconds, my guilt would turn nauseous and I'd have to run home. But, braving it, I did wait and wait for him outside the train station, with my mobile primed to take a photo. Six, seven, eight times I waited. Probably just as often as I went next door. But either I missed him in the crowds or he went a different way (or he was on a different train, now that I think about it). And I suppose I should say I listened for him, too. Maybe a month or two back I'd rearranged things, so that my bed is now against the wall between our rooms. Could barely open the door, but never mind: we're sleeping so close that I can almost touch him. There's nothing between us but plaster and brick, probably not even a foot thick. Not even an arm's length. I lie against the wall at night. I hold my hand to it, press my ear against it and listen, listen, listen …

Listen, Stephen, I must have tried to take his photo two or three dozen times: in the rain, in the evening light, on weekends, outside his house, and in the high street. But he was never there. Or I wasn't there when I should have been. So, when I finally see him in his garden, leaning against the fence and staring away at nothing, I want to laugh. I'm not even ten metres away and bent nearly in two, pulling up the weeds that had grown through the patio gravel after all the work I'd done months before. I didn't care that the garden is looking ragged again: all I'm really doing is trying to keep clear of Mum; and I want her to see that that's what I'm doing. She's through the window, in the kitchen, preparing a meal that I know I can't begin to eat. I'm angry with her. I didn't want to tell her I don't feel like eating – or at least I know I can't tell her why – so I'd gone into the garden, to where she would see I'm in a mood, sulkily pulling up weeds.

I think dinner was her 'famous' lentils and sausages, a recipe I knew she'd nicked from Nigella. That's what it smelled like anyway.

So yes. M— is leaning against the fence and staring away at nothing. How long had he been there? Why doesn't he say anything? Has he seen me? Have I done something wrong? Maybe he's angry with me because I kept ringing his buzzer and running off? Maybe he's had enough of me? I think he must know that I've shifted my bed to be near his and he's fuming about it, repulsed by it. Maybe he's heard me at night when I smooth the wall between our beds and whisper to him, always keeping my voice as soft as his. All I know for certain is that he must know I'm in the garden. He has to. You couldn't miss the sound of the gravel rustling beneath me. And I've been purposefully noisy about everything too. Just so Mum would see that I don't want to eat.

If that makes any sense at all.

But noisy as I am, M— doesn't move. His shoulders are clear above the fence: the perfect photo. Utterly perfect – but so perfect that I think my sudden silence will make him spin round to see why I've stopped making such a racket. When I pull my mobile from my pocket I worry that he'll hear the gasping little snap of the shutter and he'll whip round and see what I've done and – then what? He'll hate me. Never speak to me again. Demand I erase it and never speak to me again. Do to me what I think he's done to all those kids – or worse. Fly over the fence and … Even if I cough over the snap, he'll spin round and see I've snuck his photo. That I'm a sneak – and an obvious, bungling, clichéd sneak at that!

But what if I take his photo and pretend I was taking it of something else? What if I take it and quickly turn the camera away? Before M— has time to turn round, I'll point it at the passion flower creeping up the drain pipe, at the rusting watering can, the garden gnome. At Mum through the window. Or at me. Just flick my wrist round the other way and …

Any will do. They're all lies and any one of them will do.

But my hands are shaking so much now that I can barely select the camera function. The photo-taking and the lying and that I'm finally going to get the photo I want. The photo that proves M— is M. The photo that proves I'm not making up things in my head, that I'm not bonkers. Silently, I swear to M—, as much as to myself, that I won't tell a soul when I find out the truth. I only hope he won't move before I get my snap.

The camera is ready.

I aim.

I crane back my neck to see the screen.

I hold it steady.

I promise myself a Wishing Well and a two quid Straight Flush if I pull it off.

I zoom.

I watch M— in the screen for a moment and – I swear it, Stephen, I swear it – for a moment, for half a second, I *swear* he starts to turn round. Not to see what I'm doing, mind, *but to see if I've done it yet.* A slight knowingness in an ever so slight turn. A fractional quarter pivot, like his eyeflash has sparked off, alerting him to me. That I'm the danger behind him. Yet he remains perfectly posed. It's almost as if he's inviting me to –

Click

And right then: 'What are you playing at?'

twelve

I haven't said much about Mum and Dad, have I? What they look like, where they worked, how they raised me. The break up and so on. I forget what I've already told you and I'm not exactly sure what I've forgotten to say. But I know I've left things out. Not on purpose. You see, I saw on telly when you traced your roots back to – was it Marburg? – and I suppose I must have confused me knowing your history with you knowing mine.

So: Mum, then. She'd remind you of someone I bet you know – and maybe another friend? Whatshername, Eddie off *Ab Fab*. The spit, except for her hair. Same curlyish brown, but Mum's, gorgeously, was all swept up in the back, like a Gibson Girl. She was always showing off her neck and she always did her best to keep her face out of the sun. She wasn't pale, but her skin wasn't aged and taut like these baked walruses you see waddling off planes from Costa del Sol or wherever. No, Mum's colouring was more or less the womanly equivalent of a magnolia-painted room. Basic. Neutral. A good selling point. And probably what hooked Dad. He was an estate agent. Mum would kill me for saying it, but I wasn't planned. She had me young. Dad was too. He was 23 and Mum 19 when they found out. Condom exploded or something. Or maybe they were just trolleyed and couldn't be buggered. I don't know, I don't know. It's not the sort of thing you ask, is it? All I know for certain is that they had me and, for a while, everything was fine. Mum took maternity leave from Macmillan HR and Dad went on being an estate agent, not that he liked it much. He never stayed at the same agency for more than a year. Acorn, Abode, Halifax, Townsends, Turners, Haart, Bushells,

Kinleighsomethingoranother, Foxtons, Streets Alive, Rushtons, Merriweather & Hatch, LudlowThomas, Wrigglesworth, Punt & Lockett … I had all of his business cards. Mum had them first and kept them pinned to the kitchen corkboard. When Dad left, she binned the lot. But I got to them before the dustmen. Because, when Dad came back, I wanted him to know I still loved him.

Then I binned them too.

No, that's a lie. I burned them. I don't want to get ahead of myself, so I'll have to come back to that one later.

But just to paint the picture: Dad, briefly. He liked kiteboarding, but never took me to Blackheath or wherever else he got off to. He was good at maths, good at fires and, for a good few years, liked making his own black pudding. If he was anything, he was C of E – not that he ever went to church, not even at Christmas. Six feet tall and the sort of ginger that any fluctuation in the temperature and he'd go as pink as a pill. Blue eyes, like mine, and a mouth as thin as his lies.

More than anything, I remember that all of his socks were brown. Does that mean anything? What would Freud say? I don't know. I don't know if I *want* to know. All I know for certain is, that's what I remember from when I was small and would crawl over to Dad, slumped and creaky-jointed in front of the telly, and pull at his socks.

He didn't like that, I imagine.

Perhaps he's changed colours now.

Maybe he even wears stripes.

But, really, I suppose, Mum and I should have seen it coming. Dad disappearing and all. It was the way he moved from job to job and never settled down. Always complaining about his portfolio, about his managers, about policies and properties and vendors and buyers and … the lot. He was never happy with any of it. Properties were just commodities to him, never homes. They were worth eighty-five grand or one hundred and eighty-five grand or two, two-fifty. Dad sold them and got his cut. When you think about it, properties are kind of like scratchcards: pick a lucky one and you walk away with thousands. Do that a couple times a month and – well!

But no, we weren't rich. Far from it. And we weren't outrageously middle class either, if you know what I mean. Kids in our street went to the comp. The brainy and ambitious went to uni and everyone else went to work. Maybe some on the dole. We said 'serviette', 'ta', and 'afters'; and Dad sounded awkward whenever he tried his hand at rhyming slang. Like he was trying to be hip, or something he wasn't born to be. We had a two bedroom first floor Edwardian maisonette with black-painted iron steps down to a shared garden, a car, three tellies, high street clobber, cylinder candles in the fire; and I got an Acer 1650 or something like that for my fourteenth birthday. Printer, too.

I had a bike. It was red.

Basically, we were comfortable. Along with Mum's salary, Dad's commissions did the trick. And sometimes, for some people, that's all you can do.

Ha! But Stephen – Stephen, sometimes the trick's on you. Dad had access to all those empty properties. He must have always been touring young single women round flats. Young women buying a place together, or young women who were buying with a man but who, like Dad, weren't the sort who'd let something like that get in the way of a shag. I can just see him in one of his boxy Next suits and a wide purple tie: 'The bedroom, no, after you, love. Now, to the *rear aspect*, the bedroom … '

Mum, even with her hair in a … in a *chignon* and her long neck on display – what chance did she stand against a younger model with a flirty fringe, her parents' money and an arse that wiggled like a dancing duck?

Like me with scratchcards, I bet Dad tried his luck several times before he picked a winner. Maybe his managers caught him at it? Maybe they nailed him for it? Complaints. Could that be why he moved jobs all the time? I don't know. All I can say, after everything I've won at scratchcards, is the money always runs out.

Always.

Yes, Dad was his way and I'll probably always be mine. But, in her way, Mum started to change when there was something like a month to go before I was untagged. Not that I think that had anything to do with how she was or why she started to change. It's rather that it was around then – maybe a few weeks before, in late July or so – that I began noticing a certain shift in, and an acceleration to, the things she did and how she went about doing them.

For starters, she became evasive. Or, if not exactly evasive, as though she was *prepared* to be evasive. Like her nerves were drawn nearer and nearer the surface. She was wired up for defence or … It was everything to do with her spending more and more time out at night and on the weekends and leaving the room whenever her mobile rang.

And yet … and yet as much as I can say Mum started to change, in a way she didn't at all.

Let me explain.

When Dad left, Mum went through a period of what I'll call Non-pellucid Despair – or NPD, as the medical press would probably have it. She did what she had to do but not much else. She went to work, went to her therapist, and tiredly kept on at me to do the washing up, chuck out the papers and all that. She came home directly from the office unless she had to go to the supermarket. She cooked. She ate.

But on weekends, she wouldn't change out of her dressing gown. Just lie in bed, or on the sofa in front of the telly. Not watching it, but staring absently into or past it, as if it wasn't there. It was on, but her eyes would barely move. She didn't talk. And if she did, her words trailed off, as though they were stolen straight from her tongue. She looked confused. Mad. Mental. Like the way she'd part the sitting room curtains and then hurry to the front door and stare at it as if she expected it to suddenly spring open. She'd forget to bathe – but when she remembered, she'd be in the bath for hours, literally hours. Even listening with your ear to the door, you couldn't hear a sound. She drank, but never seemed drunk. Just empty, maudlin, exhausted, and utterly-utterly bored and incapable of so much as blowing her nose or brushing her hair. In fact, once, after she'd been lying on the sofa for something like six or seven hours, her eyes about as alive as your shoe and her hair all split and oily, I saw a bluebottle land on her ankle and practically *stroll* right on up to her knee.

Mum didn't even flinch.

Well, I wasn't about to just sit there, was I? I smacked it dead with a rolled up magazine.

Mum couldn't have thought much of that. But at least it got her off her arse. She went right past me, slowly upstairs to her room, not saying a word. You couldn't hear the door close, but there was no missing the detonative sob from behind it.

It went on and on. You could hear it in every room. Even outside.

I read somewhere, or maybe saw on telly, something you said about depression. You said it helps to remind yourself that it isn't your fault, that you're not to blame and that it will pass.

I didn't say as much to Mum.

I wish I'd said something.

But I didn't know how. So I simply kept out of her hair.

How? Mostly by staying in my room and only emerging when I needed the loo or something to eat. Or when I'd convinced myself that winning at scratchcards would somehow – I don't know, *cosmically* – turn Mum's life around. That the lucky card would cure Mum. I was generous about it, sacrificing any potential financial winnings for the big-big payout of Mum going sane again.

Other times I'd sit in the hilltop park, under the tree I always liked for its views, telling myself that Mum just had a headache, cramps, or was getting the flu. But you get a feeling about these things, don't you? My gut told me there must be a lot more going on than I knew.

Which, of course, was the case. I wasn't there the day Dad left. I was at school. So I don't know what was said – or if anything was said at all. All I remember is coming home and finding Mum at the top of the garden steps; I don't think I ever realised before how steep they were. I was in my tie and blazer and Mum looked like she'd eaten glass. She was holding the railing so tightly that her arm shook right the way up. Her hair was waving in the wind like some sort of mad semaphore and her feet were bare. Dad was gone. He didn't leave a note. He didn't say goodbye. The corkboard with all of his business cards was still hanging in the kitchen. It was gone by breakfast. Mum said we had to move. She couldn't stay in 'this house'. Every day was empty and emptying. I don't know if there's anything more to say.

Sometimes we're like the clouds. We resemble something that's not truly there – animals and faces and things. Other times we're like ... well, we're still like the clouds. Only it doesn't matter what we look like, we just get blown away.

But, by and by, we find our form again. We get better. Mum started looking after herself. Or at least she stopped being so sad. She saw her therapist three times a week – and, after a while, three became two. I started stealing things and not giving them back. We moved house. And that's when I knew Dad was really gone.

Gone.

Like I say, three became two.

Just Mum and me.

But then, I had to wonder. Something like a month to go before I'd be untagged and Mum started to change. Sly, subtle stuff that I didn't really notice at first. Like spots on your bum. One day it's as smooth as custard. Next time you look and – pop-pop-pop-pop-pop – bloody Braille back there. All the changes in Mum must have been cooking away and cooking away for some time, from way back when, in her NPD.

Biological, isn't it? Evolution. Change. Pure and simple, it's simple biology. And expensive. I'm not just talking about everything Mum bought or spent money on, but also the emotional investment she must have plonked down to even get herself in gear.

Something was up. Something was going down.

The pencil skirt was one of the earliest signs. The skirt didn't suit her. I advised her against it. Petrol blue didn't go with her skin tone. And it was too tight on her thighs. Mum ignored my advice – or at least she kept the skirt: *chacun a son goût*. But more and more, she would ask what I thought about her new purchases. She never asked straight out, but sneakily eased into it, usually starting off with something about work, something in the news, or asking what I'd like for dinner.

'We can have chicken fajitas, but only two each. They say people are too fat these days … And did I tell you I've been thinking about a dress I saw in the window of …?' Or, 'We're interviewing for three new regional managers this week, so I've got to look smart. That angora cardigan I showed you, do you think it would go with the cream camisole I …?'

Similar stuff with toiletries. Mum was always one for pampering herself: she had little pots of creams, little tubes of oils, masks and wipes and something approaching a whole apothecary of scrubs and ointments and exfoliators and … Basically it was enough to keep a boy busy for days. I gave everything a whirl. Whenever I was bored, or for any reason felt I deserved it, I'd head straight for the bathroom cupboard and would massage Mum's unctions into my cheeks and forehead, below my eyes, up my arms, around my elbows and hands, my chest, under my chin …

What I'm saying is that I always knew what she had on the go. It was never anything special. Not until July or so, when she swapped L'Oreal for Lancome, Neutrogena for Elemis, Tesco's Finest for Eve Lom, Garnier for Clarins. And, to my delight, at least half a dozen things from SKII's new skin-tingling, pore-cleansing, eye-brightening, top-of-the-shelf range.

Mum smelled great (and so did I).

We were clean.

We were cleansed.

Bright as a blush.

What else? She got a new Blackberry; it was as light as a petal. A new Blackberry, two or three new handbags (including the burgundy-coloured leather one, from Marni, that was practically large enough to carry *me* inside, let alone the secrets she was keeping in her matching new wallet and her new mobile phone), and jewellery. Personally, I don't like too much jewellery on women – and none at all on men, for that matter – but Mum knew what she was doing. The necklaces were simple, often knotted, just a string of beads; and the rings were kitsch chunky things that looked at once playful and posh. The earrings – the three or four pairs that she held to her ears, asking me if they went with what she was wearing – you wouldn't ever notice because all you saw when you looked at her was the arc and matte of her neck and the great, curling, upward sweep of her hair.

Her hair. You can always tell a woman's mental state by her hair. The week CCTV footage of M saving Sam Kulawanea hit the news – in fact, I think it might even have been the same day, otherwise I'd have thought more of it – Mum had her hair dyed. She didn't need to (there were only a few greys, and they looked dignified on her, much like yours do on you) but she had it dyed all the same. Dyed, cut and sculpted.

… And with it, any lingering bitterness, any dormant sadness, was lifted right away. Lifted right away right away. You could see it in her face: an insouciant, practically seraphic glow. In how she held herself: with a girlish, almost impish ease. And you don't need to be a Shakespearian scholar to see it in the text messages she was sending me:

> Gne shopping in town!!!
>
> Pizza 2nite? Order in: £ on dressr xxx
>
> Out for drinks home by 1!
>
> In taxi home xx
>
> Bck late!!!!

It's not as though I kept a record of this sort of thing, but Mum was spending more time on the phone. If I poked my head into the garden, where Mum liked to sit in a deckchair beneath the honeysuckle, she'd always have her mobile with her, texting away or turning it over and over in her hand. If we were watching telly and her mobile went off, she'd check to see who it was before going upstairs to take the call or rapidly texting back, swift as a sneeze.

Don't think I didn't try and get the score! I mean, *please*. Mum went to the loo and I went for her bag. Mum was doing the washing up and I was stealing across the sitting room, to wherever she'd left her mobile. Mum was in the bath and I was in her room …

But she was too clever. Her mobile was always locked. Try as I might, I couldn't crack its code.

Why didn't I simply ask her who she was talking to, who was texting her, sometimes after midnight? Truth is, I simply couldn't. I couldn't have asked her any more than she could have told me outright.

No, I needed something more, something solid before I could do anything.

Yes, Mum had her secrets and I had mine. But I did find something out. Rooting through her giant handbag for some scratchcard money, I found a wad of shop receipts. If I was Dad I'd be able to add them up lightning fast. I'm not Dad, but I'm no dope. Mum had spent something like £600 in the past few weeks alone. On what? It was right there in her wardrobe, in her chest of drawers, and under the bed. Four new pairs of shoes, three tops, skinny jeans, sunglasses, a fat brass bangle, and a flouncy bra and knickers set, still with the store tags bound through the labels by little plastic loops.

Funny thing was, none of the receipts were for restaurants or bars. Not a one.

So who was paying?

You understand, Mum was going out two, sometimes three nights a week. Out to dinner, out for drinks – and on weekends she'd sometimes be out in town for hours and hours, sometimes all day. It must have been pretty uplifting for her to have so much to keep her entertained. But did she say a word about it? When she did it sounded vague, dismissive, as though she was holding something back. Or like she didn't know what she was doing – not exactly – and so couldn't bring herself to talk about it in detail.

Worried me no end.

Not just that Mum might be in danger of going mental again, like she was setting herself up for another crash, but also, bizarrely, that I found myself in the strange position of wanting her home at night. *I* didn't want to be there, of course, but, somewhat perversely,

I needed the assurance of knowing she was safe indoors. She was out and I couldn't sleep – at least not straight away. It was the man in the woods. If something like that could happen to me on a summer's evening, before sunset, just imagine what would happen to Mum, tic-tacking home in her new heels, after dark, alone, and too brave or too careless after a few too many drinks.

I thought what had happened to me is exactly what would happen to her. But worse. I don't know what I would have done if Mum had not been home the night LOCK Crazy Crew tore into Neville Stubbs.

It'll sound insensitive – or should that be incendiary? – but after I knew she was safe that night I … well, I *resented* her for it. I didn't resent her safety but … I was all cut up about M—, you see. And that Mum could just swan off to work the next morning as though it was any old day, leaving me on my own to go wild, agonising about M—. Well!

Yes, resentment, Stephen, I admit it. There it is. Resentment in its most beastly, most bewildering strain. Resentment and, as a consequence, shame. And ludicrously misplaced, even fantastical, anxiety. This is the … the *triumvirate* of mutinous, stir-crazy emotions that grips me, after a full day of terrifying myself that M— is mortally wounded or in hospital and alive only by the grace of some bleeping modern-day iron lung, or has been chucked into jail for the second time in as many months, when I skulk, into the garden. Not so much to kill time and allot myself at least temporary clemency from everything that's plagued me for the past eighteen or more hours, but to demonstrate irrevocably to Mum that I not only can't be bothered to eat her 'famous' lentils and sausages, but that I am also – quite frankly, thank you – *in a mood*.

More aggravating yet, Mum, duly and surprisingly (I couldn't decide which drove me craziest), holds up her end of the bargain and comes home directly from work and launches into the two or more hour task of preparing dinner. She waves me hello from the kitchen window. In response, I chuck a handful of dirt and dandelion onto the newspaper flattened at my feet.

Do I over-egg it? Do I, by my sulky insolence, actually *invite* Mum, if not into a riotous confrontation regarding my attitude and manners, then at least to venture outside to see what's bothering me? Equally, do I exaggerate to you? Perhaps both, perhaps neither. Mum went about preparing stock for the lentils and I (however defensively it sounds) have to say that this is simply my warts and all recollection of everything just as it happened. And you can't get any closer to the bone than me. I was right there for all of it.

Right there.

Only a stone's throw away. Just as near the centre of things as M— was from me when I saw him the evening after Neville Stubbs was very nearly beaten to death only a few doors down.

You'll remember I said that M— was standing the other side of the garden fence, seemingly leaning against it, and staring away at nothing. And you may also remember the sudden lightning strike of delight I felt upon seeing him. A pure rip of exultation that tickled me to the point of having to stifle a laugh. M— was alive, he wasn't in jail, and he was standing so perfectly upright and still that I could now get the perfect photo of the back of his head, even if I'd have to take it from below rather that above, like it appeared on CCTV.

Which I do. I take the photo.

Right when Mum, out of nowhere, with simmering disbelief (and a witchy wooden spatula in her hand) goes: 'What do you think you're playing at?'

'What,' I reply magniloquently, 'do you mean?' And I'm so humiliated that I go gelid.

Mum points to where she's standing. 'Over here. Right. Now.'

'Wha-at?'

Mum doesn't say anything. She just stares, as I'm certain M— is staring at me now too. Although I'm too embarrassed to look at him, I have some notion of his presence, and only know for certain he hasn't slipped away when I hear Mum address him by name, gently, the same as he might say it, in a voice as preposterously soft as a mousse.

And then – as though I actually need any further evidence that Mum's changed or is at any rate chang*ing* – she does something I didn't think she'd ever do. Or at least something I didn't see coming.

'Give it here,' she says, holding out her hand for my mobile, 'and go stand over there.'

Mum points to the fence, to where I see M— is still standing. Only now he's looking over the fence and into our garden, at me. His eyes are ringed darkly with sleeplessness, regret and worry.

And me? I'm ninety-eight point nine per cent embarrassed and one hundred percent over the moon. Grinning away like a dirty little fool.

So there we have it. Maybe it's no Cartier-Bresson or anything, but that's the photograph. Not the one I wanted, not the one that would prove M— was M (that photo, the one I took, was a horrible blur). But the one I have now, still today: the only photograph of me other than my mugshot, from back when I knew M better than anyone else in the world.

thirteen

FEET OF A HERO.

Awful pun. But do you remember the headline? It was front page on the *Standard* and the *Metro* and *London News* and that other freebie paper people in bright windcheaters used to thrust at you outside train stations. Big photo of M's feet. Or not his feet, but his shoes, passing in the upper fifth of the frame, on the pavement across the way from the CCTV camera above the Budgens in Hollyhock Lane. It was 30 July; and by the following morning, something like 3,000 people voted in the YouGov poll asking if these were the feet of M.

Three thousand people. Three. Thousand.

I don't remember the results, but that's hardly the point.

Suffice to say that most people said: Yes, it's M. And all of the papers – even the serious ones, the ones you probably read – covered it. Photos, poll and everything.

Don't get me started on the online stuff. The telly: Do you recognise these shoes? cried BBC London, reporting the poll results. It was their top story. And I don't know if you recall that news presenter, whatshername, the tangoed one always in the leather skirt, interviewing the police inspector? He confirmed they'd identified the make and held up a pair on camera.

But then Gok Wan or some other said they were a different shoe. Both brands sold out of stock like *that*. Overnight – literally overnight – and you couldn't buy a pair anywhere. Or anything even *looking* like them. They were trading for three hundred, three-fifty online. Everyone who was anyone had a pair. Bed-headed indie band bassists. It girls with big feet. Chavs smoking spliffs in the park. Self-promoting DJs. Television reporters recreating the scene. The cops had to break up a girl-fight in a shoe shop somewhere – Oxford Street. Or was it Croydon?

Doesn't matter. Point is, for those of us following M (and I was by now far from alone) it was gold. Pure-pure gold.

But the shoes. Truth to tell, you could barely make them out. The CCTV footage was grainy. It was shot at 2:23a.m., that same night Mum took the photo of M— and me in our gardens. The shoes were light brown brogues, size 11 or 12, laced at the front, with a scalloped heel. They came to something of a point, rather than a rounded toe.

Same or similar shoes M— wore the evening he saved me in the park. Same or similar shoes Rabbi Fuglewitz reported seeing. Same shoes hundreds of men must wear to work every day.

On 30 July, Denise Kyte and Derek Hemmings were assaulted in Ferriers Close. Police speculated they were followed from the moment they got off the night bus, at the stop outside the Budgens, in Hollyhock Lane.

Denise and Derek were chased, sandwiched between parked cars, and beaten with bricks. Beaten in the face, back, chest, arms, and head. Everywhere. Nothing is stolen. Police find foot-long dents across the bonnet of the car the assailants are pulled from beneath. Denise and Derek are unconscious and propped up against one car; their attackers are beneath another. Hoods ripped from their necks, eye sockets ballooned shut, wrists shattered. Their fibulas were broken with such savagery that they not only cleave through the skin, but take some meat right along with them. Like kebabs.

And their faces, chests and backs marked with big letter Ms.

Just like the papers. M. M. M. Just like all over the telly, websites and blogs.

Just like my head, if you could have seen inside. You see, it was about then that I discovered M— wasn't going to work anymore. At least not to his job in IT.

Bombshell! And as though that wasn't enough, the other cracker was – suddenly – I now had only one month to go. One month before I was untagged. One month till I was free. Free, free, free – in only thirty-one days. The final seven hundred and forty hours of a five thousand seven hundred hour sentence, of which more than two thousand were spent in court-ordered, court-enforced, tedium-inducing, nocturnal quarantine and abeyance. Not to mention all of the hours I spent travelling to, sitting before, and returning from Darrell Thomas, in his dank, urine-scented and smoky office.

Are you looking for work?

Would you consider volunteering?

What's on your mind?

How's everything at home?

Do you realise how troubled you look?

Why don't you just say it?

I think you do – I think you know just *what I mean.*

… And I would grunt, shrug, squirm, deflect, tune out, dispute, disengage, and lie.

Just about the only thing that I was happy to talk to Darrell about was my studies: I was cruising, so to speak, blazing along. Did I mention how I got top marks on my mock feature article, 'Cognitive Dissonance and High Street Hysteria'? Or how the university said I was definitely one of two or three students they were looking at recommending for a work placement with Zandra Rhodes at the Design Museum?

You could see it in Darrell's face – a pride of sorts – and in the way he nodded solemnly when I boasted to him about my studies. His approval meant the world to me. After all, it wasn't as though there was another adult man in my life. Apart from M—.

Did I have a fixation or what? A fixation, a crush – sometimes they're one and the same. Synonymous. But suspicion is something different. Make no mistake: I suspected M— was M.

That is to say it wasn't just fantasy and guesswork anymore.

No, when I saw M— from the top deck of the bus my suspicion-ometer shot straight to red. Doesn't sound suspicious? Well, let me tell you, it was something like half-two in the afternoon when I saw him slipping anonymously up the high street. I was returning home from Darrell Thomas's, and there was M—, heading past the butchers and video shop, sifting swiftly toward god-knows-where.

Or on the trail of whom?

But here's the kicker: it was warm. Not only warm, but practically hot, and the temperature was rising with each passing minute. (You do know that four is typically the hottest hour of the day? All the hours of sunlight mean the temperature rises until four or so, at which point things begin to cool, owing to the declination of the sun. Quite interesting, no?) And what is M— wearing, but his long, dark coat buttoned right to the throat.

I won't con you. I only saw him for a second – two at best – before he disappeared beneath the butcher's striped awning. Was there a flash of red from beneath his coat? If there was, I missed it. What shoes was he wearing? Couldn't tell you. All I knew was, it was him.

How did I know? How did I know it wasn't just someone who *looked* like him? Because the first thing I did when I got off the bus was run. It's not just that I was wary – or, if truth be told, so terrified that I'd get these hammering headaches whenever I so much as *thought* about nipping out for a scratchcard – it's not just that I was wary of running into my attacker, but also that I was so certain it's M— I saw, that I was all abuzz to double-check he's really not home.

I ring his bell, knock the knocker. I'm bricking it. Keep looking over my shoulder and figuring out which way to run, if there's anything I can use as a weapon. But I don't leave M—'s front step until I've rung his bell half a dozen times and banged and banged the little brass knocker practically right through the door.

Nothing.

Not a thing.

He's not home.

So: it was him. *Him*. When he's supposed to be at work.

Which is exactly what I think he's up to: getting down to business.

For the rest of the afternoon, I've got no choice but to sit by the front window and keep watch.

I don't see him. I keep lookout for something like four hours, until Mum comes home and distracts me by asking what I'm doing, peering down the street. There's something funny about her voice. Edge. It's as though she isn't asking me *what* I'm doing, but if I've done something. Or if, in fact, I'm half-hidden by the curtains and searching the street to see what *she's* up to.

By the time I finish making up something about, I don't know, seeing a chatter of parakeets swooping about, I figured M— could have already slipped past. So I pack it in.

But only until after dinner. When I go for it.

I won't bore you with the details – trust me, they are boring: mainly hours and hours and days and nights of me watching and listening – but instead go straight ahead and tell you what I discovered.

Three things:

One: M— definitely wasn't going into work any more. Try as I did, I didn't see him again (not until he came and saw me, for tea, the last time I would ever see him alive). But that in itself tells you something. You see, I watched for him from before dawn, when there is only you, the morning stillness, and hundreds of robins twittering in the trees. I never once saw him leaving for work. Early bird, worm: bollocks.

Two: M—'s garden gate, I think I mentioned, opened onto the copse that ran behind the houses all along our street. Scared me senseless, but I went and had a peek back there. Follow the copse along to one end and it dumps you out at a littered enclosure with something like a dozen tin-door garages: a depressing and squalid storage yard, mainly disused apart from fly-tippers and kids spray painting everything and all. Cracked asphalt, oil stains, old mattresses. A right dump. At the other end of the copse, the one nearer M—'s and mine, there was a slumped wire fence with a chained iron gate, separating you from the narrow alleyway between the card shop and the Indian on the high street. Curious thing was, while the chain had seen better days – it was as rusted and scraped as it was heavy – the padlock was brand spanking new. I wondered, and would find out soon enough, why.

But right, getting back to M—'s garden gate. You almost never saw him in the garden, but sometimes the gate was open, sometimes shut. I kept an eye on it from my bedroom window. Sometimes I thought I was going mad when I heard it creak after I'd switched posts really quick-like to have a peek out the sitting room window, or when I finally packed things in for the night and flopped down in bed. It was almost as though I was being watched. Like someone was waiting in the copse, keeping quiet, keeping still until I disappeared from view.

Three: M—, quite simply, was still living next door. I know this because the lights in the front of his house were on, often late-late-late, and they'd be flicked off at different hours every night, meaning he was there and that he wasn't getting much sleep.

This seemed to corroborate his not going into work. Unless he was an insomniac, I don't know how he could have done both. The lights in the front room, and only ever in the front room, were on sometimes until two or three, throwing a slanting needle of light through the curtains and across his little front garden. But you'd dash to the loo for a sec and – like that! – total dark.

Why? I'll tell you. I figured it out. The lights went out when he came home. When exhaustion all but broke his narrow frame, he dragged himself home to recharge and to remind himself of his purpose (and of what he was reduced to). He would refuel with the few bites he permitted himself to eat; a few hours of melancholic sleep. And also through drawing on the wretchedness which I imagine feasted on him, as much as he on it, by the pitiless fact that he had to recoup between the very walls that were only recently inhabited by everyone he loved. The same walls that were the mute witness to the frenzied attack only months earlier that had rendered him bewilderingly obsessed, isolated, and murderous. Alone.

Which is why he left the lights on. He wanted it to appear as though someone was home. Someone home, waiting for him when he returned.

And yet … and yet I remember thinking: he's avenging Tara and his parents? Don't be ridiculous, it's too *easy*.

Or too bloody difficult.

You choose. But M— was definitely hunting LOCK Crazy Crew day and night. Definitely.

Same goes for everyone after M. It was exciting to see it go all fox and hounds. It increased his value in a way. And made me jealous. It felt as though I was in some sort of abstract competition for M—'s attention.

Thandie Burnett, whose boyfriend Kevin Wallace, if you remember, was stabbed to death that June, said 'Enough was enough' and appealed for M to turn himself in. So did Rabbi Fuglewitz who, in his singsong double bass voice, dismissed instantly any notion of M being a golem.

Boy X's mum went way beyond that. She held a rally on the steps of the library, denouncing the police for their 'inability and intentional inaction' in capturing her son's assailant. And that was …? M. M, she said it was M! The crowd erupted, chanting *M-N-O, M-N-O NO to M, NO to M*. More than a thousand flyers were distributed. There was a fight at the nearby Burger King. Two people got stabbed.

Bill Derwent, the motorcyclist who M rescued from the hit and run, studded his leather jacket with a giant letter M, and posed for the paps in front of City Hall.

A letter from 'Outraged' appeared in the local paper, saying: *I take it that Cllr Woodward, with regards to her ongoing support for planned policing cuts, coupled with her Fat Cat taxi allowance and her annual salary that she voted to double, takes the taxpayers as blind fools. When it comes to gangs and maniacs like M running riot on our streets, we have the likes of our dear Cllr to blame.*

The Chief Superintendent addressed a meeting of local residents, encouraging everyone to 'build bridges' with young people, whom he encouraged to 'break the silence' and 'stand shoulder to shoulder' with the police to end the 'needless violence'.

Which, apart from being so hopelessly impregnated with clichés that it was almost bereft of any meaning, was kind of funny. Because the rumour going round the Interweb was that M stood for Metropolitan Police. The Met *wouldn't* catch him, so it went, because he was one of them. A secret non-lethal hit man, sanctioned to clean the streets of gangs by the commissioner, the Home Office, the Justice Department, the Masons – and, of course, Prince Phillip, too. Why not Lord Melchett while they were at it?

And if you think *that's* laughable, it was enough to make you pull the plug on your Mac if you saw the one about M coming from Mars. Or the Top 10 M songs (as voted by 380 people). Or the speculative casting calls for who'd play M when his story became a film. (By the way, if it does, I wonder about you producing it?) Or the bookmakers' odds on M's arrest: after CCTV captured him striding purposefully up Hollyhock Lane, they dropped from 35-1 to 11-8.

Or something like that.

But, you ask me, the odds didn't look so hot. Not until police recovered the rotting body around the corner, maybe two hundred metres from where I was, by now, all but studiously ignoring my studies to watch for M— day and night.

No, things didn't look good for the police. It wasn't only the rising violence and the unsolved deaths which dated back six months or more to the evening of the triple murder next door and leading right up to the corpse quite literally up the road, but also M, the logo, all over the map.

Nobody could have predicted it at the start of summer. No reason to. But now you saw the letter M on everyone. You've seen pop stars with things scrawled on their arms or wearing statement t-shirts for charity. Well, it was like that. Young people started writing M on themselves. Why? To look dangerous. Or 'street', sort of like with electronic tags. Or to look like victims, maybe. Like victimhood gave them a heightened identity. Credibility. Depth.

Did you catch the photo of that blonde kid with the M tattoo across his six-pack? Huge, wasn't it?

But the real letter M, the one centred high on the chest of M's cardinal-coloured top, was small. It was hardly larger than the polo player or alligator you see on expensive shirts – or at knock off prices at the market. His M may have been small; but M, the unlicensed brand, was massive. Market stalls from Camden to

Portobello to Brixton to the Walworth Road shifted their wares by the hundreds and thousands.

M on baseball caps and t-shirts.

M on wallets and knickers and jewellery, jackets and jumpers.

M on babywear, knitted hats, scarves, wristbands … even hooded tops and bandanas!

But get this clear: there was only one M. His logo was everywhere, but there was only one of him. I don't care what anyone says; nobody else did what he did. But how he managed to … It's a wonder how he managed to do it at all. Half-eleven he rescues someone over by that giant cemetery, or in the estate where the dog track used to be – twenty minutes later and he's at it again outside the abandoned cinema, miles and miles and miles away. Christ knows he couldn't fly. Taxi drivers would have shopped him. He's there one minute, gone the next, off somewhere else. Bing, bang, bong. Like Dad.

Where M— had his top made, I don't know. Perhaps some far-flung cousin working for pennies halfway around the world, or some stooped and ageing aunt in Bradford, knocked it together for him? Maybe he whizzed it up himself.

I dare say I never saw as much as 2p for my design. But let me come back to that later.

For now, I hope you don't think I'm upset about it. Please don't. It's too late for upset. Or honour. And anyway, the point is that the police were right up against it, what with letter Ms worn by everyone on everything, everywhere. *Where's Wally* times ten squared. Where's M?

You'd have to hope the cops were looking twice as hard for LOCK Crazy Crew. Not just some small specialist unit like Operation Trifecta or whatever, but the whole force, from across all of the postcodes where the gang indiscriminately raped and robbed and beat people to death. They did Jalander Ghosh. And David Dickens. And Marcel Henry. And, months and months too late for it to make any difference to him, the police finally said they believed it was LOCK Crazy Crew who did M—'s parents and Tara too.

And then:

On 4 August, at around 10:30p.m., they followed Thomas Weir and Sadie Davidson, 29 and 28, into their ground floor flat in Berwick Grove. They punch Sadie unconscious and rape her in front of Thomas. It's the last thing he sees: they stave in his face with the same iron bar they used to beat Sadie between the legs. Spray paint their chests and backs and the walls with LOCK. For what? Know what they get? Kicks. And a clean seventy quid.

On 6 August, at around 11p.m., Imram and Aarya Abbasi, 34 and 30, were speaking long distance to relatives in Pakistan when they were attacked with baseball bats, a shovel, and a knife from the butcher's block beside their sink. The video posted on YouTube shows three assailants beating and stabbing Imram and Aayra and carving LOCK into their faces, backs and chests. Takings? £60, a laptop and two mobile phones. Their screams were heard as far away as Lahore. Both bled to death.

Three nights later, Mum didn't come home. At 10:46p.m., she texted to say she had had to work late, gone for a drink, and would be staying at a 'friend's' near the office. She said she'd explain later.

But I didn't know how she'd even begin.

You see, her mobile phone statement had arrived earlier that day. I'd taken the liberty of opening it.

fourteen

Where shall we go from here? Where shall we go? There must be half a dozen ways. Probably more. So many squirrelling and snaking together, in fact, that you'll have to forgive me for thinking everything happened all at once.

It was like the buses: you wait and you wait for hours in the rain and then the whole bloody fleet shows up out of the blue.

So, maybe I'll just stick with Mum's mobile phone statement. I found it in the hall, face-up on the rough coir mat where the postman had dropped it through the letter box with all the rest of the bills. I was out when it arrived, otherwise I would have found it sooner. I'd raced home from Darrell Thomas's, eager to see if M—'s gate was open (it was shut when I left), or if he was anywhere in the garden. The post, and Mum for that matter, was the last thing on my mind. But I remember feeling a certain righteousness when I began peeling open the envelope – a sense of righteousness, ingenuity and trepidation, if I'm honest, but a sense of righteousness most of all. You see, I felt I had a right to know what Mum was getting up to. My future – or at any rate, my future for as far as I could see – was dependent almost solely on her.

I worried for her safety. I worried she'd get beaten and raped. Or killed. Or again assaulted from within, by that something that would kick her adrift, into an immobilising stupor, where her one buoy, if you will, was her criminally convicted 'poof' of a son, me, her very own electronic tag, of sorts.

So I really didn't think much of opening her post. I'm sure it wasn't the first time. Or was it? Yes, I think it might have been. Maybe. It's difficult to remember all the little facts. But the main ones… I've said Mum was going out more often and had become increasingly private. Although she never said as much, it was evident – or likely, if you prefer – that something like two years after Dad ran off, she was seeing someone. The same person for whom she left the room to phone and text, and who had no qualms about ringing her all hours of the night.

Mum's mobile statement was six pages, front and back. She'd made something like two hundred calls, sent three hundred texts – most of them to two numbers, a mobile and a landline. The mobile I didn't recognise (and I can't for the life of me remember it now, even though I memorised it that day), but there was something that I suppose *nagged* me about the landline. Something familiar and yet slightly-slightly off. Like I knew it, but it had changed by a digit or two.

Or like it was a number I'd seen in an advert somewhere but had never dialled.

So I dialled it.

I rang them: Coxswain & Malefice Estate Agents.

I rang him. I called Dad.

He may have left, but Mum, it seems, didn't leave him. So now do you see how she changed but, in a way, didn't really change at all? I don't want to turn this into one of those psycho-analytic confessions you see all over the telly these days. People grasping for their fifteen minutes because they were in some way 'deprived' of something when they were five, ten, sixteen-years-old and so now weigh-in like two and a half yaks, or can't work, or drink fifteen dozen alcopops a day.

So I'll just say that all I'm really saying is, no matter how angry she was, no matter how sad and distraught and, for that long stretch, immobilised by NPD, Mum never left Dad.

And – yes, yes – I suppose I hadn't either. Or to slice thinly the distinction, I was holding out giving up on him. I still had his business cards. They were in the bottom of my wardrobe, bound by an elastic band, alphabetised (rather than memorised); and I would flick through them to read aloud to myself on days when I was feeling low. Or really, on days when I felt like feeling low.

Dad had worked at Coxswains something like, I don't know, ten years earlier, sometime before Major or Blair or BT re-jigged the London dialling codes. 0181 became 0208 and the rest of your number stayed the same. I'd never before rung Dad at that particular agency. He was still around in those days and always came home at night, so there was never any reason.

He didn't answer when I rang him that afternoon. I didn't leave a message either. Just mumbled something about a wrong number and hung up when she answered. Some woman calling herself 'Tammy', if I remember. Did Tammy know about me? Did Dad tell her I might ring? Did he know my number? Did it register on screen? Was Tammy on the lookout for my number? I switched off my mobile and didn't turn it on again for hours.

Why? Because, Stephen – I mean, who could think of a thing to say? Who could possibly think of a single thing to say?

Well, I did. By early evening, like any peppery reporter worth his salt, I'd whetted my line of questioning to razor point. Mapped the whole thing out. Picture it: the two of us seated either side of the kitchen table, a pot of tea, my A5 spiral notebook open on my lap and pen in hand, I interview Mum, telling her it's part of my coursework, an assignment from class.

It was the only way to get to the bottom of things.

And I suppose I relished the drama of it too.

ME: Are you happy where we live?

MUM: Yes. Yes, I suppose. There are things I'd like to be different, but overall we have it good. Not too far a walk from the station and the shops and –

ME: So you're not considering moving?

MUM: No. Though there is all the crime.

ME: Does it frighten you?

MUM: No – not in an everyday sort of way. It's just that... you're aware of it.

ME: Is crime – or fear of it – something you think about when you leave for work in the mornings?

MUM: No. I usually think about everything I've got to do that day. (*Produces Blackberry from her handbag*)

ME (*Ignoring Blackberry*): What about when returning from work?

MUM: Sometimes. But like I say, it's not something that's at the forefront of my mind.

ME: And at night?

MUM: We keep the doors locked. (*Laughs nervously*)

ME: But when you're returning home at night – then?

MUM: No, not really. It's the same as before.

ME: Do you go out often?

MUM (*Blowing into her tea*): Sometimes. I have a son. And work has been rather full-on of late, so …

ME: But you still find time to go out.

MUM (*Curtly, with a rising note of defensiveness*): Yes.

ME: What do you do? What's a good night out?

MUM: (*Looking at her nails*): Oh, the usual. Food and drinks with friends, that sort of thing.

ME: With anyone in particular?

MUM: Various places. Zizzi, Pizza Express, Auberge –

Me: Fine, fine. But any*one* in particular?

MUM: Where is this going?

ME: Just answer the question. Anyone in particular that you go out with for food and drinks?

MUM: I don't think that's any of your –

ME: Oh, but I think it is. Do you see this? (*I produce the mobile phone statement from where it's been hidden in my notebook.*) Do you see this, this number here? Do you know who that is? We could ring it, if you like. Find out. No? Okay, what about this number here? You *do* know whose number it is …?

MUM: …

ME: You said before that you were happy where we lived. You said that it's close to… 'transport links and the shops'. You stated that you weren't overly fearful of being victimised by crime – not in the mornings, the evenings or when you come home late. So why, considering your geo-domestic tranquillity, have you rung an estate agency – one *particular* estate agency – no less than what? No less than thirty-six times in the past month?

MUM: …

ME: Are you thinking about moving? Or is it that you're seeing Dad without telling me. The question is for how long? That's the big question: how long? How. Long. How long have you been seeing him? How long have you two been in touch? How long were you planning to wait before telling me? Do you talk to him about me? Or maybe my name doesn't even come up? What do you tell him I've been up to? Have you told him how I've got my studies on and that my grades are good? Or do you just stick to how I got arrested and tagged and all the rest? Did you tell him why? Is he disgusted with me? Are you? Maybe you're waiting until they untag me before giving me the shove. So Dad can come back without me in the way. Without his poof of a son here to disgust him. Is that the plan?

If it was, I was fucked. It was 9 August. Meaning I had only twenty-two days to go. Trouble was the last thing I needed. The last-last thing.

The body. I know I've mentioned it, so I'm going to tell you about it now. Everything. The secret stuff. Police found him – it – round the corner, in one of the garages in the storage yard at the end of the copse behind Stillman Terrace. It was the morning of 10 August, when I had bang on three weeks to go (and still no word from Mum after she'd stayed at a 'friend's' for the night).

A junk dealer, hired to clear the next garage but one, reported a smell and an abundance of flies buzzing so loudly that they 'sounded like a jet ski'. The body's wrists were bound by shoelaces; and it was hanging by a dog lead, affixed to a bolt in the low roof – a roof so low that the body hung only inches above the floor, cleared in the centre, below the decomposing corpse, from the debris that was otherwise piled everywhere. Old chairs, a clapped-out sofa, car magazines and porn, beer cans, chests of drawers, take away boxes with desiccated chips and pie crusts ... only thing left was the urine-bleached faeces that had slipped from the body's trousered legs.

If there was anything that suggested it wasn't a suicide, it was that the garage was locked from the outside, though the keys were inside, on the floor, like they had been placed tauntingly in eyeshot of the hanging man as he writhed to suck his final breaths.

But then anyone, even the victim, could have done that. There was a slender gap between the garage door and the floor. From the inside, you could slip your hand out and snap the padlock closed practically as easily as you could lock up from the outside. You didn't need a key.

Now. Now, Stephen. Here's the truth. Here's what nobody knows but me. What the police didn't know, I wasn't about to tell them. I didn't want trouble. I didn't want to get involved. And what I knew is that the body was the man who'd attacked me in the woods.

It was him. Definitely-definitely him, I saw, when the 24-hour news stations aired his photograph. And then, of course, the man's wife made a positive ID. Easy enough: his wallet was in his hip pocket. It's partly because of her, his wife, let me say, that I don't tell you his name. She was inconsolable and didn't court the media, shunning all interviews then and since. Poor thing.

And also, let it be known, because I've never been able to bring myself to say his name aloud. So there's really no reason to start today. I will say one thing though. He was a nurse. That's what he did.

It doesn't make any sense at all.

But going by the flies and the rot, the body had been in the garage for several weeks. In fact – and I remember this – the police said it could have been hanging there for months.

What a strong dog lead it must have been.

But now, what a lead for the police! They issued a statement that afternoon, saying they were treating the death as suspicious and that, owing to the obscurity of the site, anyone involved was likely to be local.

That was the official line.

But what you found *on*line, my dear Stephen, was much-much more. Jackpot. The proverbial. There was the 'unconfirmed' report (reportedly coming from within the Met itself) that footprints were found in the dust on the garage floor. The man's own, another I forget, and a third: size 11, with a scalloped heel and thus potentially matching the pair captured on CCTV in Hollyhock Way.

I raced up the street to see everything. Front row seat and all that. But the cops had the place taped off: you couldn't get any nearer than the drive that led back to the row of garages. I sniffed; it was already hot out. The sun was blazing away and, morbid as it sounds, I wanted to see if I could smell the body, what death smelled like.

No joy. I couldn't smell a thing at all … at all *putrid*, I suppose. Only cigarettes from a few of the reporters, and the scent of soil baking in front gardens. Cut grass and fresh tarmac. Roses. The place was packed out. News vans, with their pneumatic aerials prodding the sky. News crews, positioning themselves for broadcast. Newspaper reporters and photographers spilled all the way up the street and in small packs on the pavement. I watched them with something like envy, trying to listen in to what they were saying, often at a whisper or with hands shielding their mobiles, to keep whatever scoop they had secret until they went on air or to print. I asked a policewoman if it was true about the footprints. She ignored me.

So I asked a reporter. It was news to him. Scribbled it down.

'Have they taken away the body yet?'

'Don't kid yourself, son,' was his harried reply. 'Another few hours won't make any difference. Forensics only just arrived.'

'What else you got?' I wanted to ask, but chickened out. Because it suddenly hit me that if the stuff about the footprints was true, the cops would search the copse for more.

They would follow them to M—'s house. And to mine.

I couldn't decide which was worse.

Hurrying home, and taking care to not look back to see if I was being tailed, I realised that for the first time in ages, I wasn't hurrying because I thought the man was after me. That he was out there, enraged, lurking, scratching his scalp bloody until he caught me alone, unprepared, and would finish me off. Funny thing is that he *was* right there. All this time, he was right there. *Had* he followed me? Had he tracked me down? Did he hang himself that night, after M— saved me? Specifically because M— had saved me, because M— saw his face and could identify him?

Or maybe it's the other way round. Did M— follow *him*? Did M— track *him* down? Did M— have, if not a tangible, then something of an omniscient hand in his hanging? Did he watch the man as he strung himself up – or did he, just like any shadow, follow him to the yard and, from the copse or crouching behind one of the hulking skips, wait for him to re-emerge from the garage? But after waiting half the night he has to have a peek, and sees the man already hanging and already dead.

Or maybe …? Something I've just realised is the man, if he got a good squint at M— in the woods, in daylight, when he would have been easy to make out (and thus easy to remember), was the only person who might have identified him. He could have fingered him. He could have shopped him. Do you see? *Do you see?* And so I have to wonder ...

Look, I've got no doubt that M— was returning from the garage when we startled each other in our gardens late that night after he saved me. No doubt at all. He did what he did – whatever he did – and he was returning home, by way of the copse, where nobody would have seen him coming or going, and ... what were his exact words? 'I've sorted it,' he told me. 'Don't be scared.'

Well, I'll tell you what did scare me. It was something Darrell Thomas said when he rang that afternoon 'just for a chat' after they found the body. I had the 24-hour news on the telly, and was online, upstairs, at my desk, trying to assemble the facts into a coherent story for class – and getting nowhere. Horace Harker all over again.

It was the questions that rattled me. How, when, why – but most of all: who. Questions, of course: the lifeblood of any decent journalist. Or cop. Questions, queries, theories, conjecture, hunches. There were too many – or really, too many whose answers spun right back at me. I had to wonder, what with the police now searching the copse and conducting a fingertip search only just down the street, how soon they would knock at our door. Wouldn't they haul me in when they saw I was on ISSP? Hammer me with questions until I confessed? Confessed that I'd 'met' and had 'reason to harm' the man, and that all of this quite possibly happened on the day he died. But, more damning yet, also how M— knew him. Thus providing the cops with everything they needed to again kick down and storm through M—'s front door.

I nearly hit the ceiling when I heard the bang at *my* front door.

But it was only the post clunking through the letter box. Another change in Mum that summer was she'd taken out a subscription to *Time Out*.

Salt – wound, you ask me.

Where was I? Yes, Darrell Thomas. He rang. After asking if I was okay (and, you guessed it, wanting to hear something in my voice that told him I didn't have anything to do with the body), he said:

'To thyself be proud and true. *Proud* and true. Do you understand me?

'No.'

'If my good friend Neville Stubbs can hold his head up, so too, my boy, can you.'

Neville? *Friend*?

'Now, do you have something you'd like to tell me?'

'No.'

On 11 August, at 12:15a.m., while police stood guard up the road, and probably dozens more were engaged in the minute search for clues in the floodlit garage yard, or were scouring CCTV tape, LOCK Crazy Crew banged through the garden door of 17 Blackcap Row. They beat Rodney Morrison to death with baseball bats and raped his girlfriend, Fiona, after ... you'll gag, but they used secateurs. Two weeks earlier, Rodney had complained to police about a group of youths causing a disturbance outside the off-licence at the end of his road.

On 12 August, at around 1:30a.m., a trail of blood led police to the sixth floor stairwell of Millward House. They found a 15-year-old boy, unconscious and de-hooded. His face and chest are marked with letter Ms. The chief investigating officer said the boy's hood had been 'sliced savagely away'. The cut on his neck isn't life threatening, but he is hospitalised for the compound fracture of his humerus, the lower half of his arm connected only by tissue. Police give him round the clock guard in hospital.

Now M, I ask you, Stephen, now M: what did he learn from all *that*?

On 13 August, at around 10:30p.m., LOCK Crazy Crew opened fire on a christening party. Nine guests were shot. Two die, including Ameobe Grant, 17, whom police believe was the intended target. A family spokesman said Ameobe had been threatened for not joining a gang. LOCK Crazy Crew steal jewellery, mobile phones and cash. Bernadette Weeks, 63, is the other victim. She was holding her new godchild when shot. She died shielding it. The baby lived.

On 14 August, video footage of LOCK Crazy Crew murdering Rodney Morrison and raping Fiona was posted on StreetVidz, Facebonk and all that. Most of it was hurried, blurred, a figure crouched in the corner, in the half-light, shielding himself; the shoulders and arms of Lester, Ommie and Carl swinging downward, as though chopping wood. And Fiona's face. And – Christ – her eyes. Her horrible, horrified eyes. Her screams.

It was set to music. The scenes from Blackcap Row were something of an intro, cutting crudely to a rap, shot in what appears to be a darkened council flat. Lester, Ommie and Carl take it in turns to charge and thrust at the camera. They are bare-chested. Just hoods over their heads. Hoods ripped free from their tops. Gesticulating, their hands shaped like guns, swinging fists, gripping their groins, and brandishing the thick chains round their necks, fastened with heavy padlock pendants. You couldn't make out whole lines. Only words: 'Solja', 'Nigga', 'Bitch', 'Paki', 'Respec', 'Ends', 'Crew', 'I' and 'M'. And 'LOCK', again and again and again.

The video lasted maybe three minutes. It had more than two thousand six hundred hits before it was taken down.

If M— saw it, I'll never know.

But I think he did. I think he must have done.

I think it must have tipped him off. Who was who. I think it must have tipped him over the edge.

fifteen

On 15 August M— came round to mine. It was 11a.m., bang on the dot, and I hadn't slept all night. Watching and listening for M—. Watching and listening and watching some more. And waiting: *God*, the waiting and anticipation that ... It bores you to the core.

M— looked exactly the same: sleepless and wired and lit somewhere inside by that goggle-eyed jumpiness that always comes when you're overtired. Or maybe that's just me. Just me and just M—. He was dressed more casually than usual; you can bet I took a good look at his shoes. They were nothing like anything I'd seen on the telly and, in truth, I can't even remember what they were. He wore narrow Prince of Wales check trousers and a tan v-neck jumper over a white undershirt that glowed brightly against his skin. He looked incredibly clean. Smelled it too. Not like anything in particular, but like a good clean man. Or rather not like just any man, but like himself. Like the man he was. Like M—.

M—. M—. M—.

God, like M—.

Sometimes, even today, when the breeze swirls up, I can smell him still. I breathe in deeply and it's like he still here, like he never left. I'm whisked back to when I opened the door, expecting the police with radios crackling and handcuffs loosened, and instead saw M—, in the late morning sun, looking as clean as a jet stream and as tired as a tree. I looked for the eyeflash, but it wasn't there, if it ever was.

So what else could I do but offer him a cup of tea? What else, Stephen? *Is* there anything else? It was eleven o'clock, after all.

The sitting room is a disaster. It's a disgrace (and, let's not forget, the monitor is in there too), so I ask him into the kitchen and follow him down the hall. Before I know it, he's ducking through the door, hovering at the table before sitting down, and I'm washing out the mugs. It might sound, I don't know, *daft*, I guess, but I'm adamant on our using the plain white ones. All of the others are chipped or stained, or have some embarrassingly naff saying on them, and so will in some way destroy the whole tea etiquette.

You've got to get these things right. Otherwise the world goes to pot.

Only the best would do – the best we had. Ikea.

It makes me go dizzy, M— coming round and me trying so hard to get everything right. I worry about the state of the kitchen; if it's as clean as I imagine his must always be. I worry about the carpet stains in the hall, if the milk has gone off (and if there's any milk left). Drying the mugs, I worry about the tea towel, wondering whether M— thinks it's clean. It's not. So I try hiding it by drying the mugs with my back to M—.

Which isn't any use. Because I drop a mug. It doesn't break, but I let loose this shriek. Not words, but a noise so alarmingly high-pitched and staccato that you'd think we keep a porpoise in the sink. But that's how it goes, doesn't it? You want and you want and you want to make such a good impression that nothing you do comes up to scratch. And I really-*really* don't care for the state of me. I'd washed my face that morning, but hadn't showered. Brushed my teeth, but hadn't bothered with deodorant. My jeans and t-shirt are clean, but I'm wearing yesterday's socks. They don't smell, but they're orange and – God, okay – have miniature Snoopy faces all over them. Does M— think Mum dresses me? Does he see my socks and think I'm a child?

So yes: I have this, but not that; I'm sailing clean on one point, but hardly that on the next. Your average 50/50 kind of day – and yet there is something making it feel like the odds are teetering toward a topple, or are already slipping down-down and away. The kind of feeling I'd always get when I knew I needed that much extra luck if I had any chance at all of winning at scratchcards.

But despite all of this – all of this *discombobulating* me – I still could have turned a cartwheel when M— shifts in his chair and starts, however quietly, to speak. I can only say I feel almost stupidly relieved that one of us can talk. So relieved, in fact, that I feel in a way forgiven.

Out of nowhere (or, I've got to think, no more out of nowhere and no less purposeful than his showing up that day) he tells me, 'That's why Tara was there, why she was over. We were going to tell them we planned to marry.'

The whir of the electric kettle fills the room, rising and rising as it reaches boiling.

'And I was late,' M— whispers dreadfully as I carry over our mugs. 'I was late.'

We don't speak. I, for one, don't know what to say. Which is just as well because it's probably all the things we didn't say that stand out the most. They reverberate the loudest. Probably then, just as much as they do today. What I mean is, M— doesn't ask me about the fight Mum and I had the evening after she didn't come home and I confronted her about Dad. Nobody could have missed it; it didn't go anything at all like I'd imagined. I didn't keep my cool. I didn't interview Mum like I'd planned.

Anyone walking past on the pavement must have heard us, let alone M—, sitting quietly on his own next door, in what was tantamount to a mausoleum.

But more things M— and I don't say. I don't ask him why he's not going into work, or even hint at him being the scarlet-clad M everyone is hunting for or otherwise want (need, if they are anything like me) to identify, to put a face to. Name, as a deity or devil. Likewise, he doesn't fix his eyeflash on me and ask if I've told the police that he could not only identify the hanged man, but was quite possibly (and even likely, you've got to think) the last person to see him alive.

We just sit in silence, looking at our hands, at the tabletop cluttered with bills and papers and things, drinking our tea.

I think he must have liked that. You ask me, and it's exactly what he wanted. In fact, I think we would have gone on sitting there, and would have foregone any sort of farewell at all, if I didn't suddenly feel so incredibly saddened for him that, before I'd even finished my cuppa, I asked if he'd like another.

Oh, and a biscuit. Or a chocolate: we had some fun-size Mars.

M— shakes his head. The slightest movement, like a toy top coming to rest after a great whirling spin that's rolling down and down until it's no longer rolling round and round but wavering languidly in the momentum of what was once circumfluent and great. Then, looking past me, over my shoulder and out the window, into the garden beginning to emerge from the shade, he says: 'I have to go.'

I can't move. Or nod, or even look his way.

And he is already at the front door when I manage to do anything at all.

I wave.

'Bye,' I say, and watch him step out into the sun.

Yes, you ask me and that's the reason why he came round. He wanted to say goodbye.

It was three that afternoon when two things happened in such quick succession that I'm amazed I remember which came first. But that's practise for you. That's dedication. That's going over the facts again and again and again. Listen, I know I keep forgetting things and so, every now and again, have to go back and add them in. Things happened so randomly, or seemed so incidental, that it was only later I could see that they were connected. So if it means we … if it means we *dal segno* for a second, I really do apologise.

All I can say is, I'm doing my best: my best to give you the facts as they happened and to keep things ticking along right through to the end. And believe you me, that afternoon two things happened that should have told me the end was right there.

First was the news leak. The police believe the 'Garage Death' (as the press unimaginatively called it), is linked with the 'violent vigilante rampage of M'. They've identified a key suspect and promise a swift arrest. It's everywhere on the Interweb.

Soon as I see it, I race downstairs and catch it on the telly. God bless 24-hour news. The police aren't saying much – and in fact it's not a proper news conference at all, only a Met spokesman, all but ambushed by journalists outside Scotland Yard. But now they've got this unmissable swagger. It's a restoration; you can see it in the spokesman's shoulders, his eyes, and hear it in his voice. Boldness. Vivacity. Maybe the police aren't saying much, but that's because they don't have to. Not now. They no longer have to plead with and prove to the public or to victims' families, or to anyone, that they're working day and night to crack the case. Not any more. They have a lead and, confidence restored, they're buoyant. They'd been dealt their ace.

So I panic.

Which is when the second thing happens.

My mobile rings.

It's Mum.

When, the other day, she finally came home after staying the night 'at a friend's', I'd left the kitchen a mess. Cups and plates and teabags and toast crumbs and great globs of jam and butter and biscuit chunks in the sink, on the countertop … all over the place. The couch, the coffee table, down the tea-trickled carpet in the hall. My bedroom. Mum walked in and, quicker than your modem, she started in on me – which was of course the reaction I must have wanted. Because, before she finishes telling me how careless and inconsiderate and selfish and 'barbaric' I am, my face screws up, I go red, and tell her to fuck off.

Mum picks up the receiver on my monitor. It's got something like direct dial to the police.

She looks at me, raising her eyebrows as though to say: 'Try me.'

I think she's serious.

So what else can I do but come right out with it? 'Go ahead, but you won't get Dad on *that*, you cunt.'

Everything kicks off.

… Some time later and we're still in tears. My throat is raw. Mum's face is swollen and her hair is a mess, and she's holding me in her arms. Mum never hit me before. And I'd never hit her. And I don't know how long it'd been since she held me like that, smoothing my hair and kissing my forehead, and saying she loved me again and again. We ordered Thai. Mum, for the first time since I was arrested, let me have some wine. I did the washing up. We held hands and watched a DVD. *Some Like it Hot*.

Mum said she'd fix everything.

Just give her time. A few days, she said.

She promised.

And I knew – I could see it, Stephen, same as I would later see it in the eyes, and hear it in the voice, of the police, when they'd identified a key suspect and so had an ace of a lead – I knew she meant it, too.

Seven days later (in which time not an hour passed without me asking myself: Is it now? Is it today?) at three in the afternoon, when the police say, however vaguely, that they've identified a key suspect in the 'Garage Death', that they're linking him directly to M, and I'm on pins and needles to see if a body-armoured police unit are kicking in and storming through M—'s front door for the second time in as many months, Mum rings.

'Your father,' she says, 'is coming for dinner tonight.'

And I'm simply over the moon about … about *life*.

This, despite everything, Mum tells me to do. Laundry, the loo, the kitchen, the sitting room, the carpets, the hall. My bedroom. And despite the stupefying anxiety I get about the cops nailing M—. My heart's going whackety-*whack*, whackety-*whack*, when I look outside, up and down the street, where there are (*of course*, I tell myself, giddy with relief) no police, no news teams, no helicopters whirling overhead.

I stand motionless in the garden, listening for anyone in the copse. Cops, cameramen, Alsatians …

Nothing. Not a peep. Everything is still, almost blissful. M—'s garden gate is shut, same as it was that morning, when I checked at 5a.m. and again half-hourly after that until he came round. After he left, I kept an eye on it for ten minutes straight, flattened against the wall beside the window in my room.

Ten bloody minutes.

Some spy I'd make!

Some detective.

And some friend. Because after checking the street, and listening in the garden and eyeballing M—'s gate, what do I do but get stuck in with everything Mum told me to do to get the place ready for Dad. First thing I do is dig out his business cards from the bottom of my wardrobe, and stuff them in my pocket. I tell myself I must be crazy, thinking M— is M. Him! He's just my neighbour, I convince myself, no matter if he is this beautiful-beautiful man. Who speaks to me. Who trusts me. Who trusts me enough to break into his house for him and to not steal from him. Who took me into his confidence about his eyeflash. Who submitted by email my superhero design to the newspaper (wouldn't he have said – if he *was* M – wouldn't he have done something then?). Who comes round for tea and makes tea for me when I go next door. Who saved me – who saved me *twice*. Thus providing me with all of the 'evidence' that I – out of boredom and loneliness and this inborn need to have a grown man to glorify in my eyes as much as in my heart – that I am compelled to cast him as the mysterious star in the great radius of violence and reciprocal heroism that not only peppered our leafy street of slender terraced houses, but also swept as far as any number of buses could take you in a quarter of an hour. Have I built him up unnecessarily? Is *that* what I've done?

Yes, I tell myself. Oh yes indeed. I tell myself I've got it all wrong. Let it go. Why? Because Dad is coming home.

Dad is coming home.

For dinner.

Dad is coming home.

He's coming to see me. *Me*.

Dad is coming home.

Tonight. Some time between eight and nine.

M—, for the first time in months, since when the days were only beginning to inch noticeably longer, and when my tagging still had the interminable proportion of a life sentence, goes right out of my head as swift as – well, whatever you like. As swift as a swift swooping home for the night.

Is that cheap of me? Am I in the wrong? Why do – and how can I – so readily forget about and abandon M—? Is it because I've simply had enough of the fruitless scavenging for clues and can't be bothered to think about it any more? Is it because I'm fickle? Inherently lazy? Is it because everything suddenly feels like it's coming at least within sight of a peacefulness that as recent as two weeks ago seemed about as intangible as the stars? What with Dad coming home. What with Mum and Dad (fingers crossed) accepting me for who and what I am. What with there being a mere two weeks until I'm untagged and everything will come alive and crisp again come autumn. That life – *real life* – is, for the first time in *my* life, ready to begin.

Or is it … is it because I have been so utterly-utterly obsessed with M— being the heroic and damned M all over the news that, paradoxically, I am somehow programmed to drop the whole thing as fantastical nonsense so completely and so abruptly that it's like … it's like how Dad dropped Mum and me? *Whumph*! Straight through the cheesecloth.

But the real question, I tell you, is this: if I've so readily abandoned M—, if I've dismissed all the 'facts' and 'evidence' that he is the M now being pursued by the police as nothing less than fantasy, farce and fallacy, why is it that around seven that evening (after I have twice dashed out to buy scratchcards, hoovered the sitting room, mopped the kitchen, mopped the loo, cleaned the sink and the bath, done the washing up, tidied my room, and showered) (and wanked), why is it that when I am collecting the linen from the washing line I am suddenly smacked icy with dread? We swing this way and that. Left-right, tick-tock: one hundred and eighty degrees at a stroke. It's like Newton famously said (and despite my repeating myself, it's no less relevant than before), for every action there is an equal and opposite reaction.

A spy, a detective, a decent journalist (and a reliably sequential storyteller, you rightly add) I may not be. But, I realised, looking over at M—'s garden gate, with a sheet half over my head and half draped over my arm, and the sun having dropped so low that it was now barely visible above the copse, Judas Iscariot I am.

My name is Charlie, by the way. Don't tell me I forgot to mention it! I guess I assumed you already knew.

What a fool I am. What a bloody-bloody fool.

Poor M—.

M—'s garden gate at 7p.m. It's shut. Latched as firmly as when I'd last checked it after Mum rang to tell me Dad was coming over for dinner, and when I needed to convince myself that M— wasn't about to be nailed by the police.

But now there's a noise in the copse. Whether I hear it before I look at, and then beyond, M—'s gate, or if I look instinctively at his gate because I hear a noise, I don't know. But there's definitely someone there. Someone walking, someone *creeping* through the trees, purposely slowly, as though trying not to make a sound. If they're coming closer or walking away or around in circles, I can't tell. Because as soon as I hear them, I call M—'s name.

The noise stops.

I call again. But I have to wait and wait for the slow and decisive tread, nimbly sidestepping the fallen twigs and leaves, to start up again.

It's the police: a specialist unit ready to raid.

The cops are in the copse!

I dash inside. Kitchen. Hall. Stairs. Bedroom. I bang on the wall, yelling, 'DON'T GO OUT. DON'T GO OUT TONIGHT!' with this swelling hopelessness that M— is still at home, changing into (I can all but actually see it) his pointed leather brogues, his long, dark coat and the cardinal-coloured top with the scarlet letter M high on the chest.

'DON'T GO OUT!' I yell and bang until, hearing the front door shut below, I thrust my head out the window to see if I'm too late and M— is already at his garden gate. Or, worse, the cops are pouring through it with a battering ram and bristling, bounding dogs tugging at their leads.

But his garden is still. It's quiet. The gate is shut.

I watch the copse.

Nothing

No one.

Not a soul.

Just the trees and the sky above it, ribboned in red, the envy of any summer rose.

That's exactly how it was.

And it's with this vision of … of *placidity*, I guess, that I, like any sleepwalker or zombie, stand at the window; looking but not really looking, thinking but not really thinking, breathing but never quite catching my breath, and sweating like you do when you're being chased in a dream.

Then there is the creak on the stairs that I don't quite hear. The soft crunch of carpet outside my room. The rustle of shopping bags being negotiated through the door, the hand on my shoulder turning me round. What I would have said to Dad I can't begin to fathom, what with the laundry scattered about and me looking as frightened as a cat.

But it's Mum – and it's twenty past seven. I only know the time because she looks at her watch and holds it up for me to see.

It's new.

It's Fossil.

It's got two hearts on its face. Which is naff. But I tell her it's nice.

'We need to be quick,' I seem to remember her saying. 'He'll be here in an hour or so.' She asks if I am all right, if I still want Dad to come round.

I suppose I nod. I might have even said yes, for all I can remember.

But I must have assented in some way, because Mum kisses my forehead, stands back and, taking my hand, walks me away from the window. 'Your hair smells clean,' she tells me. 'You're almost ready.'

We stand beside my bed, on which she's rested the shopping: paper and plastic and gold and blue and white bags, a small mountain in all. I think she must have taken the afternoon off, there's so much there. How she managed to carry it all home, I'll never know. She'd been to the supermarket and an easy half-dozen clothes shops. No surprise, but different this time, because one of the bags is for me.

Mum leaves and I get dressed:

New jeans, a white cotton shirt, striped canvas belt, and a light v-neck jumper of merino wool that the sales tag calls 'sage' and, embarrassingly, 'petite'. It's funny how incidental details stick with you, like a knob-headed marketing knob's word for green. I suppose it only sticks in my head now because, with a mixture of elation over Dad and guilt about M—, when I slip my head through the jumper and transfer Dad's business cards into the pocket of my new jeans, I remember that I am already turning toward the mirror to see how sharp I look.

Yes, it's funny how little things stick in your mind.

You ask me and you really do have to hold on to the little things. They're the sort of thing you never want to forget. Where you were when you were first kissed; how the air smelled of buttered toast and honeydew melon when you first fell in love; the way bumble bees bobbed in the potted lavender that first evening you sat on your very own roof terrace; and how a certain word for advanced education always makes you think of terrapins and turtles.

Or someone's email address. I remembered M—'s right then and there. His tan jumper that very morning and my new green one, practically identical but for colour and size, and I, catching sight of the darkening copse and brilliantly lit skies, remembered, out of nowhere, that I have M—'s email address. Right there. In my room.

You remember, of course. Remember that he emailed – just that once, maybe two months before – to say I got his vote for my superhero design. I'd never written back. I didn't have the guts. Not even to say thanks.

But I dash an email off now. Half thanks, half SOS, it couldn't be more fitting. DON'T GO OUT! is all I can think to write. I wait and wait for a reply. I listen for a knock on the wall. I stare at the screen. I hit refresh. I check the sent tray. Has it gone? Is it stuck in draft? Is there a delayed bounce back? Has he replied? I send it again and I'm about to send it a third time when, bang on eight, Mum calls upstairs for me to help her in the kitchen. I am tasked with slicing the carrots and celery and peppers, unscrewing the wine to let it air, while Mum peels the potatoes, parboiling and rolling them in fat, seasoning and dressing the chicken and getting everything roasting lickety-split.

While I watch for police to come storming through M—'s garden, Mum pours olives in a bowl and puts the bowl on a salad plate for the stones.

While I listen for anything sounding like M— closing his front or garden doors, she spoons taramasalata into a ceramic dish, rinses and tosses a salad, whips up a vinaigrette, tuts to herself when she sees she's forgotten to chill the cheesecake in the fridge.

And while I am reduced to staring at the wall, as though this will somehow transmit some sort of warning *through* it, Mum cuts her finger slicing pitta bread.

Do you know what it feels like to be severed in two?

There is M— and there is Dad and there is me, caught in between, trying to hold myself together in front of Mum. I don't want her to crack.

She's trying her damnedest. She's doing her best. Roasts were always Dad's favourite. The hors d'oeuvres will probably go largely uneaten, just something there for us to awkwardly nibble at over the first drink. I've seen Mum bang together a dinner that leaves the kitchen looking like a bomb site, but never so clumsily as she does tonight. Nerves. That's why she cut her finger. Her hand is shaking when she holds it under the kitchen tap.

Mum tries turning away, but I see her hand all right. She's no more successful than me, that very morning and in the exact same spot, trying to hide the grubby tea towel from M—. She is just as nervous. Just as adamant about getting everything right. Mum and me: I suppose we really are alike in a lot of ways.

But not every way. Because as soon as she rushes upstairs to change (she's bought herself some new clothes too) and to fix her make-up, I look at the cooker and I look at the hob and, necking a glass of Mum's wine, I look at the clock.

It's a quarter to nine. Dad's here any second.

I have less than two weeks, barely more than three hundred hours to go.

Or more precisely, I have fifteen minutes.

I figure Mum can always answer the door.

M— taught me a lot of things. He taught me about civility – and about mania, about madness. He taught me to hold and to present myself with dignity and pride. From him I learned, for the first time in my life, a thing or two about love (and the things you'll do for and because of it); and also, I guess, how to demonstrate dignity, love, pride, civility and, well, the lot of it.

He taught me all of those things. Maybe I didn't know it yet. Maybe it wasn't until later, until after he was gone and everything had time to sink in, that I could say I learned anything about any of that at all. But what he *did* teach me and what I needed to know now was how to break into his house through the little transom window out back.

It was the only way. I go out the front and Dad will be there. He'll stop me. Or I'll stop myself. No, I have to break in to warn M—.

I don't care if I come out alive.

Very quietly, I slide the backdoor keys out from where they're kept hidden in an empty spice jar and undo the bolt. I do the same with the little pencil locks at the top and bottom of the door, undo the chain, listening and listening for Mum on the stairs or the ring of the doorbell.

There's nothing. But still I stop. Because, trying to be silent, I'm reminded of the noise I heard earlier in the copse. What if they're still there? What if it's *not* the police? What if it's the same gang who broke into Neville Stubbs' house? LOCK Crazy Crew. What if they're there, watching? Waiting for me to open the door. Waiting for me to leave. Waiting until Mum is alone.

But Dad, I tell myself, will be here. He'll protect her.

Dad: he'll be here any minute. Once he is, I can't leave. I can't do what I have to do. I don't want to be in when he arrives. I want to be *back* – as swift as a swift swooping home for the night. Back to the whir of the electric cooker and the scent and sizzle of Dad's favourite meal roasting away.

I turn out the kitchen lights and hurry along the fencing, to where there's a loose trellis panel, and I squeeze through into M—'s garden. I check to see if his gate is still closed.

It is.

And it's probably because I'm thinking about him, here in the stillness and dark, that I imagine what it's like to *be* him. I ask myself what he would do; and I answer: *Become the darkness. I am the darkness. I am M.*

Silently, I creep over to the lean-to, stretch up and test the transom window; until now I was certain it would open like it did before. All I have to do is slide my fingers under the base of the frame, at the corner, and pull gently upward and out, straining on my tiptoes to keep hold and to not let it slip and bang back in place.

Or make a sound. Any at all.

I'm in luck. The latch is still broken and the window opens smoothly, without so much as a creak.

I keep on my toes, holding the transom open while I hoist myself up – first on the little door handle and then, shifting my weight off it, by reaching through the window and holding on to one of the thin aluminium strips that separates each of the lean-to's panes. I look around me.

I look to see if Mum's watching from the kitchen door, if M—'s neighbours on the other side are peering down from their windows or up from their garden. And if anybody's watching from the copse.

Nobody.

No one.

The only thing I see is I have to hurry. I have to do it now. If I don't slide inside this second, I'm going to run out of time, or I will talk myself out of it and I will have betrayed M—. I will have let him down. I owe it to him: he would do it for me. *I am the shadows. I am the darkness. I am M.*

Careful not to swing my feet through the glass, I squeeze forward and up and in. My arms, my head, my chest are clean through when my jumper catches on the latch. I twist and hunch and wriggle to lift it away. The latch scrapes down my back and I have to stop again, because I can't remember what I'm supposed to do next.

Breaking in was easy in daylight – piece of piss. At night, it's a blind man's game.

Half in and half out the window, I wave my arms in the dark, feeling for the something on which I know I'm supposed to steady myself. What was it? What did I use before? The stacked garden furniture? The upturned birdbath? The smooth handles of the spades and rakes? I reach for the wall and find it, the simple iron clothes hook, screwed into the brickwork and from which hangs oilskin jackets and a bonnet-like sunhat.

It's enough.

It held me before.

The hook has just enough strength for me to lever myself in through the window. Half upside-down and straining, I grope for something solid on which to stand. A box, the arm of a chair, a disused table … anything flat from which I can scramble off and onto the floor.

And from there cautiously forward, deeper and deeper into the tight, darkened lean-to. Whether my eyes have adjusted, or if a sliver of moon has risen from behind the copse, I don't know. But I can see more easily now. Shapes: the neatly coiled curves of the garden hose, the dull glint from the watering can hanging from a hook further along the wall, a bicycle, terracotta pots stacked like Russian dolls, a little storage freezer beneath boxes filled with cleaning fluids: dozens of spray-nozzled bottles and aerosol cans and, if I remember from before, more boxes yet, with empty Mason jars, rubber seals, yellowed recipes cut from magazines and clasped with miniature bulldog clips, and a heap of dust rags: scraps of thick cloth in every colour.

It only takes a few steps and I am at the French doors with the whitewashed panes. The handle is cool to the touch; so cool that it feels clean, in a way. There is an unmissable scent of cleanser in the air, as though wafting up from the boxes and buckets around me. And that's all I need to be reminded that somebody lives here. It terrifies me. If M— is here, if he's inside, has he heard me? Is his eyeflash bursting, sending him to red alert? Does he know it's me? I might be anyone: I might even be *them*. Back for more. Back to finish him off.

I also think it must be getting on for nine.

But I don't have time to check. I'm here. I have to do it. I have to warn M—. I need to save him. I want him to know it's me and that I'm here to help, so I call his name, quietly, through the crack between the doors. 'M—,' I say, 'it's me. It's Charlie, M—. It's Charlie, it's me.'

No answer. The doors stay firmly shut. I think M— must be deeper inside, in the kitchen or the front room, sitting quietly, talking to his parents in his head and waiting, like I'm supposed to be waiting for Dad, for Tara to come buzzing the buzzer at the front door.

Where *is* Dad? Where is Mum? Why isn't anyone looking for me?

I want to peek outside. But I hurry along instead. Turning the handle on the French doors, I step into the strange little box room that I can picture is the way I saw it before, in daylight, empty but for the noisy Victorian wallpaper: fleur-de-lis and crowns and garlands, red on red.

The air inside is cooler than in the lean-to. Darker. It is pungent with chemical cleansers: lemon and bleach and pine. As though the floor and the woodwork have been recently washed, scoured, disinfected. That's just the word: disinfected. Because it smells as though something surgical has happened here or is about to take place. The little box room smells so utterly clean that it smells *sanitised*.

I creep forward. The room is small but feels larger in the dark; it's as though I'm going deeper and deeper into the whole of the house while not actually leaving the little box room. My arms are outstretched and I step tentatively, like I'm testing the floor is real, that it won't suddenly open up or tilt sharply downhill. One step, two steps, one step … My fingers are shaking, and my arms are so rigid that they ache right up to my neck. One step, two steps … I must be in front of the interior door by now, so I reach out even more: slowly-slowly-slowly waving my arms in front of me, until my fingers brush against something not at all hard like a door, but something soft and supple – sending me reeling backward into the corner, cowering.

The walls are soft yet firm. As though padded. I can feel the softness through my clothes. When I reach out it is there again on my hand: the empty, cottony texture that I prod and then run my fingers across and forward and down and forward and down and up and up, feeling the differing fabrics that are all baggy and smooth – until my fingers find something small and solid.

I flick it and blink in the sudden bare-bulb light. And because of the sight.

I am surrounded by hoods.

They are everywhere, stabbed through with drawing pins on all four walls. Black hoods. White hoods. Blue, green, checked, grey, copper, patterned, and purple hoods. Hoods coloured deep-deep artery red. Hoods with frayed threadlets dangling like tiny veins. Hoods cut cleanly or ripped savagely away, flecked with blood and hanging there as though waiting to be filled, waiting for heads. The walls are blanketed so densely with hoods that it is impossible to see the noisy red wallpaper that had before filled the room's empty space.

It's a long time before I can move.

And I think I only do because I hear a mobile ringing. At first, I don't know it's mine; I think it must M—'s, on the other side of the door, because the ringing is muffled and some distance away. I crane my neck and listen, following the rising beep of the ringtone away from the interior door and back the way I came, through the French doors, into the lean-to, where I see my mobile upside down on a sunbed. It must have fallen out while I was wriggling in. I don't know *what* would have happened if I hadn't found it.

Same with Dad's business cards, which I see fell from my pocket and onto the floor.

The phone call is Mum. But I don't stop to talk or even switch off the ring. I know she must be worried. I know she must be thinking I've run off because I'm nervous about Dad. I know what she will ask: not only where I am, but why I'm not home, now, at 8:58p.m.

Two minutes.

I pocket my mobile and Dad's cards and don't stop to think about what to do next. I hurl myself into it, shoving aside the sunbed, the rakes and spades, the stacked garden furniture and boxes, and the giant charcoal grill that rattles so loudly I worry it will collapse and clatter like a gong – all the while trying to count down from 120 in my head, but having to stop because I'm running out of time and all of the counting makes me jumpy – until there is a path leading from the lean-to door straight through the French doors and into the little box room full of the hoods that I can feel staring down at me with this spitting hate at the injustice of what I am about to do.

But before I can do it, I have to see to the lean-to door. It's locked; I know I'll never find the key. But I've done this before. I did it when I stole things and never gave them back. The lock is minimal, it's basic. No more substantial than something you'd find locking a child's toy chest. Climbing atop of everything I'd pushed to the side, I aim my foot to strike cleanly on the handle. The little lock pops free on my second stamp with a pleasing little ping that I don't have time to savour, because as soon as the door swings open I have already leapt down and am back in the little box room.

There is something sad – something outrageously sad – about the hoods. In their tens and dozens, their sheer spread and height, they have the pretence and flair of an art installation, like something designed to visually demonstrate the vast numbers of crimes and criminals and victims. But what's really sad is what a great sense of failure they must be to M—. Not mistakes, but simply the wrong people. Near misses. It's like trying to find someone to love and who will love you right back: nine times out of ten you think you've found them, but there's always some point in the early hurried tangle of love when you see you've cocked it up again.

Right or wrong, I began tearing down the hoods and running in to the garden with armful after armful, piling them up and up until they are in a heap as high as my chest. The smell – the many-scented disinfectants and cleansers and sprays absorbed in the dozens and dozens of hoods – hangs in my nose and waters my eyes and clings to my new clothes.

I said that the little box room smelled like a hospital, like something surgical happened there. But when I see it's the hoods that carry the scent as much as the floors, the door handles and the wood, I think something else. I think something worse. I think something happened to Tara in the little box room. One by one, or maybe all three at once.

It's where her body was found 'away from the others'.

I think M—, by using the hoods to scrub the little box room over and over, was trying to cleanse her.

And, Stephen, if it doesn't sound overly grand, that's just what I wanted to do for him. When my phone rang earlier, I knew M— couldn't have been home. I knew he was out and that I couldn't warn him. But I thought I could save him. Not only from imminent arrest and jail, but also free him from the palliative monstrosity that didn't so much eat away at him like a disease, but that he, in every way, had absolutely become.

And like M— with Tara, it is the cleaning solutions that will do it. They make the perfect propellant. The long-stemmed firelighter I find hanging by a lanyard from the giant charcoal grill; if I didn't find it there, I'm certain there would have been one – a box of matches at the very least – in the kitchen.

I don't know why I even mention it.

Maybe it's because, upon finding the fire lighter, I think that I am so incredibly intuitive and clever to know almost by instinct exactly where to look. Or, now today, so unbelievably naïve to not fully realise M— left it there for me to find. That it had been placed.

When I return for the last time to the little box room to turn out the light, I notice something I should have seen before. But what with all of the hoods and then, once I'd cleared them, the noisy red wallpaper, I had missed it in my haste. Hanging from a miniature hook screwed into the woodwork framing the interior door is a little wire ring with two padlock keys.

They could be for anything. For the bicycle in the lean-to. For a garden shed that has since fallen down and been removed. They could have been hanging there for years. Forgotten about. But they look new. So I shove them in my pocket and scramble outside, into the garden, where, with a can of wood polish, I set the hoods alight.

They burn and they burn. For how long, I don't really know. I didn't stop to think. But what I can tell you is M— must have used can after can after bottle after jar to maniacally clean that little box room again and again. Because the hoods don't smoulder. The flames leap up, crackling and spitting and splintering right up at the night sky as though trying to claw it down to earth.

The whole garden was alight. And the billowing black smoke, thickened by the witchy chemical brew, swirled along the backs of the houses, through open windows and high above the roofs. Perhaps that's why I removed the elastic band from Dad's business cards and scattered them in the flames.

You see, the smoke was so caustic and so heavy, and the flames so noisy, so intense and so bright, that when I looked over and saw Dad wasn't the other side of the fence, in our garden, yelling for me to stop, or simply mute and incredulous at the sight of me standing there in the light of the blaze, at the edge of the flames, coughing from the smoke, with a can of propellant in one hand and a firelighter in the other, with an electronic tag on my ankle and it now well after nine, I knew – I knew, Stephen – I knew that he wasn't going to come.

He didn't.

But someone did.

Someone came.

M—'s garden gate was unlatched. It was wide open.

sixteen

On 15 August, at 4:30p.m., while he was conducting the day's penultimate viewing of the double-fronted, four-bed Victorian house with sash windows, wisteria, and a south-west facing garden at 78 Haversham Road that was valued at something like £500,000 (and so would have earned him upwards of ten grand), Dad, despite his embarrassed and then enraged protests, was handcuffed in front of both his clients and the prospective buyers and whisked away for questioning on suspicion of murder.

The police held him for seven hours. Held, fingerprinted, photographed, needled, cajoled and interrogated him, until he was probably as furious as he was scared. And it was only minutes before nine when he was finally allowed to ring Mum. She, in her new skinny jeans and new carmine slingbacks, with her hair freshly swept back and pinned up to reveal her lightly-scented neck (and with the roast sizzling away and me already edging deeper and deeper into M—'s horrific little box room) hurried to the police station in a taxi frantically flagged down in the high street. It was all for naught. Because when Dad rang, he not only told her he wouldn't be coming round for dinner, but also that he didn't want anything to do with us again.

I think he meant me.

I think that's what he really said: that he didn't want anything to do with me. Only Mum would never tell me that. She never has. I don't think she's ever been able to tell me the truth, that when Dad rang he told her he didn't want anything to do with me. And because of me, Mum too.

It was my fault. I was to blame.

You see, the police believed it was Dad who murdered the man – the nurse, of all things – who had attacked me in the woods. Dad was their ace of a lead. That was what the news conference had been about. That was what came up, in detail or not, when they grilled Dad before finally releasing him without charge. They told him why he was there, why they suspected him, why they had reason to believe he had sufficient motive to execute the man from the woods. They told him what happened. They told him what the man did to me. Yes, that's right. They knew all about it.

And when Mum arrived, they told her too.

It must have been the police. Either them or Dad's solicitor. Dad wouldn't talk to Mum. He wouldn't even see her.

And I can only think the police didn't talk to me first – or really, to me and to Mum and to yet another solicitor she would have had to get because of me – to verify what had happened in the woods because who would we tell (so they would believe) but Dad, straight away, thus giving him time to work up an alibi or simply disappear.

Much like he did – like he did twice. I've never seen Dad again. Estate agents: love them or loathe them, you'd be mad not to loathe them.

No, the police had to act fast. With certainty and in full view of the general public, hungrily following everything on air, in print, on the radio and online twenty-four hours a day.

Does that make sense? It does to me. Although sometimes, when I think about it, I have to raise an eyebrow. Sometimes both. It sounds too crazy, too amateur and ... You have to understand just how much of a bollocking the police were getting, what with all the unsolved murders and rapes and street attacks and video clips and CCTV clues and M de-hooding every other kid in sight. Everything kicking off and everyone hounding them to get their arse in gear. Wouldn't the police have made *dead* sure they got it right? Headline stuff like that, I know full well from my journalism training, and you've got to get things spot on.

Mum? Me? What did the police want to know about our movements the night the man disappeared? Not much. Mum had an alibi: Dad. She'd met him for dinner out. Which, of course, was his alibi, too. I was at home, under the eyeball of the monitor and tag. We were in the clear.

Besides, I suspect the cops didn't rate us as murderers. The man was something like six-two and had more than three stone on each of us. Mum and I are petite, as my new jumper would testify. We couldn't begin to string up a heffalump like him.

The real question though, is who. Who talked to the police? Who told them what happened to me in the woods? Who rang them with the anonymous tip that not only fingered Dad as the key suspect, but also dished out enough detail of my attack to convince the police that Dad had the incentive to avenge it by murder? Who would do that? Who?

Who do *you* think?

M—, of course, didn't know Dad was coming to dinner the same day that he himself came to say goodbye. I never mentioned it: it was coincidence. Him shopping Dad was a decoy, M—'s clever-clever way of distracting the police away from the copse and away from his door – through which they would have entered in force and found everything they needed in the little box room to crucify him – before he could finish what he needed to finish, if only to feel some sense of release, some sense of justice, before he disappeared forever. The police were *that* close, literally yards away. All M— did was distract them. He gave them Dad's name. So buying himself the few hours he needed to finally confront and mortally punish LOCK Crazy Crew.

On 16 August, the day after I'd broken into M—'s, the front page headline read 'MET-RAGEOUS' and inside was a six-page exposé of the police's 'bumbling, negligent and at best casual' investigation of M and the 'plague of street violence'. The paper condemned, not only the Met's 'severe inability' to curb the rising numbers of attacks, but also its 'bald-faced contempt for every man, woman and child who they are categorically failing to protect'. It was a tabloid, of course. They called the Met 'sloppy'. They called it 'slapdash'. Victims' relatives wanted compensation – piles of it. Head teachers, local residents and councillors were quoted. Photographs of young people showing off their neck wounds and broken limbs, CCTV stills of M intervening in the attack on Sam Kulawanea, and of him stealing, lightning quick, up Hollyhock Way were enhanced, blown up and reprinted in a two-page spread.

And now, as further evidence of the Met's 'systematic failure to perform even basic investigative duties', there were photographs taken inside the garage where the man was found hanging, and of the copse that ran from the garage yard all the way along the back of Stillman Terrace, where the paper 'uncovered vital clues overlooked or ignored by investigating officers'. Snapped branches, clothing fibres caught in tree bark and fencing, and footprints that indicated not only 'frequent and almost certainly daily' traffic through the trees, but also that someone wearing pointed and scallop-heeled size 11 shoes had habitually lingered out of sight, within only a stride or two of a garden gate. M—'s, in fact. As though spying on the houses.

The photographs were taken only the day before. I know, because I'm in the background in one of them, taking down the linen from the line. My back is to the camera, I'm not exactly in focus, but it's definitely me. I know what I was wearing. The same hooded top I had on the day M— told me about his eyeflash after he attacked me in his front hall.

So, unless the tabloid returned after dark and for some reason decided *not* to snap me breaking in next door, decided *not* to photograph me running wild-eyed to and from M—'s house with armful after armful of hoods and setting the tremendous pile of them alight, I can only think it must have been M— who unlatched the gate that night. He returned home one last time but, seeing me, he quietly watched from the shadows as I incinerated all the evidence that would damn him, much like he must have watched me from his bedroom window months earlier, when I trimmed and weeded our garden so that it might begin to look as tidy and prim as his.

I mean, who else could it have been? Who else could it possibly have been? Why, if it wasn't M—, didn't my photo, in full light of the fire, appear in the paper the following day? Why didn't whoever it was ring the police? Why didn't they ring the fire brigade? It was him: it was M—. It had to be.

I know it. I know it, I know it. Stephen: I *know* it.

But why did he come back? Why risk it? If he was dead set on disappearing, if his job was done, why come back? Was it to check on me? Was it to see if I was doing what he, in some way, must have known I would do? How long did he stay? Did he leave the gate open on purpose? Did he want me to know he'd returned and left – or that he was *there*? Did he want me to see that he was watching? Was it a signal, a signal to get out, to get away right quick? Or was his unlatching the gate the same as leaving open a door for someone the other side of it: did he want me to follow him?

I'll never know.

The things I've done. The things I wish I'd done. Everything I got wrong. Oh God. Oh. *Oh God* …

On 17 August, police found three bodies in Flat 612, Tranquillity House, the easternmost block of the sprawling Byron Estate. The bodies were arranged carefully on the floor of the empty sitting room. Two have their heads pointing away from the front door, and the other is positioned the opposite way, face up between the other two.

That was Ommie, the smallest of the gang, and the only one of the three whose limbs weren't bound tightly to his sides. His bare legs were spread wide, at something like 45 degrees, so that the tips of his toes touch the heads of Lester and Carl. You don't need to be a genius to see that LOCK Crazy Crew were arranged to form an M. A scarlet M: their bodies, stripped to their punctured, slashed and broken skins, were painted in blood.

Lester, Ommie, and Carl were drained – purposefully drained (so the tabloid press reported some detective or another stating) – of enough blood to 'float a child in.' Which in the eyes of the law they were – children. Lester was lashed and strangled with a thin, rubberised cord. Carl was battered in the face, neck, chest, groin, and back. Ommie was slit and stabbed. He was opened up. Lester's and Carl's jaws are shattered. Six of Ommie's teeth are down his throat. All of their knees split. Ankles like jellied eels. And their bodies are stripped, bound, fixed into position and mopped over with blood, front and back, and across their faces and necks and right down to the balls of their shattered feet. Lester's, Ommie's and Carl's bodies, you understand, were as bare and as red as the walls of M—'s little box room.

And their hoods were missing, too.

I can't claim I saw their hoods hanging from the walls. But I have to wonder if they still made it on to the pile before I set it alight. Maybe ... maybe that explains the open garden gate.

I only thought of that now, otherwise I would have told you before.

But I have, I know, told you about the superhero design I did for the local paper. The design I showed M—. It was black on black, if you recall, with the letter U set within a five-pointed star. M— may have changed the colours and, in a way, lost the star (he never wanted to be one,), but I can still see it in what he chose to wear on his chest. The five points of my star were for each of the five postcodes where M had rescued someone or stopped a crime. You ask me and M— kept the star. Only he converted it to the first initial of his first name.

Do you see it? Count them out: there are exactly five points to the letter M.

M— was like that: we were friends. It saddens me to think I was the only person he had left who he could trust. He left little clues for me to piece together. Clues to who he was and what he was doing. And why. He told me things. Not always in words but ... Think about it: three things. First is the day he came over *specifically* to show me how to break in to his house, he was only pretending to be locked out. It had been raining, absolutely hooning it down all the time he wanted me to believe he had been trapped outside. And yet there he was when I answered the door, as crisp as the icing would have been on his wedding cake. Marzipan.

Then there are those keys I found in M—'s little box room. Remember that padlock I spotted on the slumped wire fence when

I braved it and went snooping about in the copse? This was before they found the body, and I was a mess, up here, in my head. The padlock was new; the chain it fastened was old. As rusted as it was scraped and heavy. Well, have a guess what those keys were for. M— didn't need them that night, because he left through my front door.

And the logo again: M— never emailed it to the newspaper. If he had, I'm certain I would have won. Dead certain. No, the paper never got it because he only sent it to me. Remember his message? *This one gets my vote*, he wrote, simply, and signed his name, M—.

Well, it certainly did. It certainly did.

And four, I think. Yes, there's definitely a four. He confided in me about his eyeflash, which, let's face it, let's be honest, was nothing more (or should that be nothing *less*?) than post-traumatic stress. PTSD. There's no such thing as superpowers. But that doesn't mean there isn't such a thing as superheroes. M—'s eyeflash, I have to believe, was a maniacal and stress-induced defence, over which he had no control. It was real enough; I'm sure he saw it the same as he described. But I have to think he saw it hundreds, probably thousands of times, when it wasn't anything urgent or dangerous. Just ordinary, everyday people and things and nothing-doing events. Someone darting for the bus or dashing from a shop. Someone popping up from their train seat. The shadow of a tree waving on his bedroom wall. He sees it – whatever it is – and his eyeflash lights off. His eyes told you everything. In the five or six months during which he went increasingly insane, and his eyeflash flared up whenever he so much as dragged himself past the little box room, he hardly slept a wink.

He was on a mission. That's what M stands for: it stands for Mission, because he was on one. And Motive, because that's what he had. M stands for M—, of course, because that was his name. And M is for Magani, just ask any London Nigerian. M is for Miseria, if you're Portuguese. M is for Mozzare, if you're from Venice, Sicily or Rome. M is for Mordować, Mutiler, Mugu,

Martiya, Marisu, according to the Poles, the French, Ghanaians, and in Romany and Japanese. M is for Mone kawra: it's what he must have heard his parents ask of him in their native tongue, after they were gone. It means 'remember'. I know; I looked it up on the Interweb.

But most of all M stands for Missing, because I never saw him again.

On 31 August, at twelve minutes to midnight, twelve minutes before I was officially free, the uniformed and taciturn team of two showed up and untagged me. They needed the monitor. Apparently, they'd run out. So they came for mine.

Mum took the monitor off the bookshelf and, with exaggerated ceremony, wrapped the cord round the box. She handed it to me, I handed it to them, and Mum held me in her arms. She kissed my head and rubbed my hair. She cried and said she was happy for me. She was happy I was free, and happy I was still there, around. It wasn't just the attack in the woods, but also that I wasn't banged up in jail somewhere.

I could have been. Definitely, I could have been. My tag and monitor should have done me in. But Mum saved me. She lied for me when the police came round the morning after Dad was arrested. Mum didn't know about me and the break-in, about the hoods and the fire. She only knew I hadn't been home like I should have been. So she did something wrong to do something good. She lied. She looked the cops in the eye and said I was home all night. She said she was too. Big risk, I know. All they had to do was check at the station and see. But she knew they wouldn't, and turned on the charm to make certain. She smiled and twirled her hair and said that she'd blown a fuse. Too many electrics all at once. Hairdryer, cooker, lights, DVD, computer, phone charger … She said she'd tested the monitor to see if it was all right and it seemed to be working perfectly fine. 'The little light was blinking. Is that not right? Here, come and have a peek,' she bluffed. 'You'll find my fingerprints all over it. In fact, the old fuse is still in the bin. Would you like me to dig it out?'

The police conferred. They said thanks, but no. That wouldn't be necessary. I nearly shit myself a moment later when Mum asked them to stay for a cup of tea.

Yes. They would like that very much. But they had to dash.

What Mum had really done, I can tell you now, is unplug the monitor straight from the wall and chuck the fuse. Night before and she gets the call: the police are holding Dad. She races downstairs and sees I'm not there. So she saves me. Pure and simple, that's what she did.

She'd lost Dad. I think Mum would have cracked if she lost me too. She needed me. After all I put her through, she needed me. She stuck her neck out. I loved her like a lunatic for it. I've never stopped.

On 18 June, two years later, I was outside the little blue-tiled café in North Cross Road when I looked up from my paper and ran after the man in the long, dark coat. It was a Saturday, so the street was buzzing, what with the shops and the market and all. But I squeezed past the buggies and kiddie scooters and caught the man by the sleeve. M—'s house wasn't his any more. He'd sold it – or someone sold it for him, sometime a year or more after I'd given up waiting to see him again whenever I visited home. Mum said she'd seen estate agents coming and going, but never saw M— or anyone she recognised. It was sold at auction for … I can't remember how much. I didn't even know it was for sale until it had sold.

When it went, I knew it was over. I knew M— was gone and that I needed to stop looking for him in crowds or for his face in the news.

But that day in North Cross Road, from the shade below the awning and with the sun beating down and the air already hot as toast at something like a quarter past ten, I saw him. I only remember the date because it became something of an anniversary. It's the day I met Nathan. You remember these things, don't you? The day you do something for the first time. Exactly where you were when you first met someone. Someone you love. Nathan and me: things might not have worked out, but we were together for a long while and we're still close friends. Nathan was at the café also, at a different table, and laughed aloud when he saw me burning red. I'd thrown my arms around the man in the long, dark coat and cried aloud, 'M—!'

It wasn't.

But Nathan kept giggling so much at my mistaken embrace and hurried retreat that he wanted to apologise. He bought me a cappuccino and, even before it arrived, I could tell he wanted to hold my hand.

We spent the day together.

And the night.

I took him out to dinner and he brought me breakfast in bed. That first night was magic. It was like a film featuring *us*, just talking and talking like there was no end to everything we had, and wanted, to say.

That's how it was with Nathan for a year and a half. That's just how it was.

My first proper boyfriend.

God, it was great. No more here's-my-number-but-I-know-you'll-never-text-me snogs, or anonymous and emptying shags. No more hiding and feeling guilty when you wank, or feeling horrible about yourself when you hear school kids calling each other 'fag'. Or, I don't know, Jeremy Clarkson deriding some car he's wrecked as 'ginger beer'. It's such a massive relief to say it, say who and what you are. Get it done with and get on with finding someone to love and who loves you as much as you love them. Everything opens up for you, opens up inside. Because once you say it, you can do whatever you like with it.

Me? I wanted to tell everyone. I needed to: I'd denied it for so long. Top of the list was Darrell Thomas. I went to see him at his office. He was behind his desk. The place still smelled of smoke and wee. I didn't go to see him because I had to, but because I could finally say what he'd been waiting for me to tell him, three days a week for the whole of the nine months he was my probation officer. Darrell, if you haven't already guessed it from everything I've told you, is gay too. It's one of the reasons he knew Neville

Stubbs. They weren't lovers or anything. They were, and still are, I think I should say, scarf-wearing Gunners season-ticket holders and tight-tight friends.

After I came out to Darrell, I went along with him and Neville to a few matches. Nathan didn't care one way or the other, but he came along too. Just to be with me, just to be together. And to drool over Freddy Ljunberg, the tart. I bought all the drinks and food. I could afford to, on account of my winnings. Scratchcards had finally paid off. I won big. BIG. Mum had given me £180 for my birthday when I turned 18, six or seven weeks after M— disappeared. She got me a laptop and an iPod too. But with the money, I bought a jacket and a couple of books, some flash deodorant from Liberty's, and a Midas Touch scratchcard that I couldn't be bothered to scratch right away (or to use my lucky 50p piece on, in case I gave it the jinx) because it was only after the shopkeeper tore it off the roll that I saw it was from the No 5 dispenser. I was certain my luck was cold.

Boy, was I wrong.

It would be crass to tell you just how much I won. But I will say it was enough for me to buy a place of my own. Buy it outright. I've got a one bedroom flat and a big ginger cat called Max. He likes sunning himself on our little roof terrace – and so do I when I can find the time. Work gets in the way; I'm no good with money, you see. The flat is about all I have to show for my winnings these days. I blew the lot. Blew it in Thailand and Sri Lanka and Crete and Sardinia, in Turkey and Barcelona and Valencia and Dubrovnik and Provence and New York and here, again and again – pretty much all the time for a good three or four years – at home. Eating out and clubbing and buying rounds of drinks and presents for Mum and for Nathan and Max. And for me, clothes and clothes and clothes. And books. And DVDs. And music. My bank account emptied out faster than a wank. I got a couple of credit cards that I ran up and up and up. Sky high.

It's no good having to work.

I don't like it. Waiting tables is boring and beneath me.

I deserve better than this. I'm meant for better things.

I'm certain of it. I'm dead sure.

Take Claridge's. Claridge's, Lord's, Ascot ... Once all of this gets out and I'm up there again where I should be, maybe we could go for high tea somewhere? Go to Brown's, or go and see the cricket and the races, quietly poking fun at the gaggles of chavs parading round in complicated hats and spray-on tans and their hired Jimmy Choos. Or go to The Groucho. Fine wines at your club. I won't hang about, or hassle you about becoming a member. It's not that I don't want to or anything like that. I mean if it's on *offer* ... You do some great things for charity. You, your club and all. And it's not like I won't have the money to pay the annual fees, or will sponge off everyone when it comes to rounds and after dinner drinks and lashings of pheasant pâté and bruschetta and medallions of rabbit and trays of Essex oysters and crèmes brûlées and whatever else is in season.

No, this will take care of all of that, don't you think? It'll sell like hotcakes. After all, it's the truth. It's the real thing. And I was really there, intimately, you might say, involved.

I've been thinking about this. A lot. About everything. I've been thinking hard. I mean, now that you know everything I know, now you know everything there is to know, I wonder how it should begin when it's a book and a film. What we should say, right at the start, to really draw everyone in. I was thinking:

'His name was M—, and he was so beautiful that I hardly heard a word he said.'

'Come again?'

Thank you

Dave, Jo, Jo, Nancy, and Ben (and Jodie and Emily and Mark and Northern Dave, and everyone else at 194): for your friendship, for the room at the top of the stairs, and for the Tokyo Suite.

Andrew and James and Vicky: for your friendship and for all of the literary advice and encouragement.

Vann and Russell, Chuck and Bill, Aaron, Andy, and John: for several hundred things (and if there's any joy, several thousand more). If you're ever feeling thirsty ...

Roland Denning: for paving the way (and not just over the beach), and for your literary and publishing advice. And, of course, for your parties.

Debra Shostak: for (very patiently) tutoring me when I was first trying my hand at writing all those years ago.

Debi Alper: for sticking up for me, for all of your guidance, and for editing and proofing this book. It's impossible to imagine things without your support.

Leila and Ali Dewji: for your faith in this book, in me, and for your tireless work to make this book everything that it is.

To my family, whom I love, although I hardly ever say it.

What did you think of *Now You Know*?

Please leave a review on Amazon or contact
Christopher Chase Walker directly through his website:

www.nowchristopher.com